"I still need to add the sugar…"

"You're telling me," Marshall replied. His voice came out in a strangled croak and he began to cough again.

Lovey pointed at him with her spoon. "Sorry. Though my *mam* did teach me to make lemonade so you could taste the lemons."

"Did she?" He laughed. He was captivated by the pretty young woman's eyes, her smile. "Your *mam* would approve of this batch for certain."

"I *am* sorry," she repeated. Then she giggled again.

Marshall watched her. "I can see I'll have to be more careful about reading signs literally when I come in here."

"Maybe you should." She smiled to herself, adding the sugar to the pitcher.

He couldn't take his eyes off her. There was something so familiar about her.

This girl wore the Amish clothing of every other local girl he knew, but there was something remarkably different, yet familiar, about her…as though he'd known her all his life. And suddenly he wanted to know her for the rest of his life.

Emma Miller lives quietly in her old farmhouse in rural Delaware. Fortunate enough to be born into a family of strong faith, she grew up on a dairy farm, surrounded by loving parents, siblings, grandparents, aunts, uncles and cousins. Emma was educated in local schools and once taught in an Amish schoolhouse. When she's not caring for her large family, reading and writing are her favorite pastimes.

Books by Emma Miller

Love Inspired

The Amish Spinster's Courtship

The Amish Matchmaker

A Match for Addy
A Husband for Mari
A Beau for Katie
A Love for Leah
A Groom for Ruby
A Man for Honor

Hannah's Daughters

Courting Ruth
Miriam's Heart
Anna's Gift
Leah's Choice
Redeeming Grace
Johanna's Bridegroom
Rebecca's Christmas Gift
Hannah's Courtship

Visit the Author Profile page at Harlequin.com for more titles.

The Amish Spinster's Courtship

Emma Miller

HARLEQUIN LOVE INSPIRED®

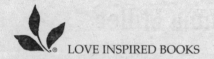

LOVE INSPIRED BOOKS

Recycling programs
for this product may
not exist in your area.

ISBN-13: 978-1-335-53909-0

The Amish Spinster's Courtship

Copyright © 2019 by Emma Miller

www.Harlequin.com

Printed in U.S.A.

Whoso findeth a wife findeth a good thing,
and obtaineth favour of the Lord.
—*Proverbs* 18:22

For my best friend, Judith.
Thank you for your confidence in me.
For your love.
You made me who I am.

Chapter One

Marshall Byler stepped into the shade of the concrete block dairy barn that housed the new Miller harness shop and breathed a sigh of relief. The July sun was hot and the day was muggy, just what one would expect for mid-summer in Kent County and sure to make the corn grow. He'd been cultivating his corn in his east field when a groundhog had startled Toby, the younger of his two horses, and he'd spooked.

Marshall had gotten the horses calmed down before they tore up more than a small portion of his crop. However, somewhere in the frantic shying of the team, Toby's *britchen* strap, a section of harness that kept the horse from getting tangled in the traces, snapped. Marshall didn't need the harness immediately, but he decided to go ahead and drop it off for repair right away, so it would be ready when he needed it again.

Miller's Harness Shop would save him time because it was closer to his farm than the Troyer Harness Shop, which he usually frequented. And he also liked the idea of giving his business to the new place; there was enough leatherwork to be done in Hickory Grove to support both the Troyer and the Miller families. Besides, the shop was owned by his new friend Will's father and it seemed only right to go there.

Marshall waited a moment for his eyes to adjust to the shadowy shop with its massive overhead beams and concrete flooring. A section of the former milking stalls had been cordoned off from the rest of the barn, and the stanchions and feed trough was replaced with shelving, display space with an assortment of items for sale and a counter with a cash register.

"Hello! Anyone here?" he called. When he got no answer, he put two fingers to his lips and whistled.

Still no response.

When he and his brother had driven into

the yard, they hadn't seen anyone around. Yet the wooden sign beside the half-open Dutch door read *Velcom* Friends. It was long past the midday meal, so where was the proprietor? Glasses and a pitcher of lemonade stood by the cash register with a sign that read Refresh Your Thirst. Ice cubes, mint and lemon slices floated in the clear pitcher, a sight that made Marshall realize just how thirsty he was. Noticing a brass bell beside the cash register, he rang it before pouring himself a glass of the lemonade and taking a deep swallow.

Marshall gasped as the strong taste of sour lemon filled his mouth and made his eyes water. He grimaced and began to choke just as the door swung open to reveal a young Amish woman in a green dress and white *kapp.* He tried to clear his throat and coughed.

"Atch," she said, and clapped a hand over her mouth to suppress a giggle. "You weren't supposed to drink that yet." She held up a pint jar of raw sugar in one hand and a wooden spoon in the other. "I still need to add the sugar."

"You're telling me," Marshall replied. Rather, he tried to reply, but his voice came out in a strangled croak and he began to cough again.

She pointed at him with her spoon and grimaced. "Sorry. Though my *mam* did teach me to make lemonade so you could taste the lemons."

"Did she?" He laughed, then choked again. When he found his voice, he spoke, captivated by the pretty young woman's eyes, her smile. "Your *mam* would approve of this batch for certain." Marshall wanted to ask her how he was supposed to know there was no sugar in the lemonade yet, but he was enjoying the back and forth too much. Instead, he wiped his eyes with his shirtsleeve. He spotted a smudge of topsoil and wished he'd taken the time to go to the house to change his shirt before coming to the shop. He also wished he'd worn his better straw hat; this one had a bite out of it, thanks to his brother's pet goat.

The woman hurried past him, putting the service counter between them before depositing the jar of sugar beside the pitcher. "I *am* sorry," she repeated. Then she giggled again.

Marshall watched her. "I can see I'll have to be more careful about reading signs literally when I come in here."

"Maybe you should." She smiled to herself as she added the sugar to the pitcher and stirred with the spoon.

He couldn't take his eyes off her. He was sure they'd never met before because he would have remembered her, but there was something so familiar about her. It was like the taste of his favorite pie. All pies were different, but blueberry had its own special flavor. This girl wore the Amish clothing of every other local girl he knew, but there was something remarkably different, yet familiar, about her…as though he'd known her all his life. And suddenly he wanted to know her for the rest of his life.

Just this morning he and his grandmother, who lived with him and his little brother, were discussing his marriage prospects. Or lack of, in her eyes. For months she'd been talking about how it was time for him to start thinking about settling down and having a family of his own. He wondered what she would think if he walked back into the house this afternoon and told her he might have found the girl for him.

The woman regarded Marshall with shining almond-shaped eyes as green as spring grass. "What can I do for you?" She eyed the leather strap in his hand.

"I'm Marshall, Marshall Byler," he told her, deliberately stalling in explaining his reason for coming. "I live just down the road. The farm with the old pear trees by the mailbox?"

She didn't respond.

Marshall wasn't in the least bit discouraged. He liked a bit of chase with a girl. "And you must be a Miller?"

She shook her head and continued to stir. *"Ne."*

He took a step forward and inspected her closer. She was tall for a woman, perhaps taller than he was. And slender as a willow. She wasn't a beauty in the usual sense, not tiny and softly rounded like his neighbor Faith King. But when this newcomer turned those intense green eyes on him, he found himself almost stunned. Not to mention slightly tongue-tied. She was sharp as a straight razor, this one, and direct in her speech, more outspoken than most of the girls around here. Deliciously tart…like her lemonade.

Marshall smiled at her, a practiced expression that had caused more than a few feminine hearts to flutter. Surely, this *maedle* behind the counter could see his charm and recognize him for the superior fellow he was? He held up the broken strap.

She seemed not to notice his smile. Instead, all business, she left the spoon in the pitcher of lemonade and put out her hand. "Let me see what we're dealing with."

"You're not a Miller?" he ventured, determined to have her name.

She accepted the piece of leather from him and scrutinized it. "This damage looks fresh."

"Ya," he admitted. "My gelding's young, still green in the harness. He shied at a groundhog and caused a bit of a panic with his teammate."

"Neither animal harmed, I hope?" she asked.

Marshall warmed to the concern in her eyes and shook his head. *"Ne,* both fine." He hesitated. "You asked about the horses, but not the man?"

She lifted her head and inspected him with a new interest, or so he hoped. "You look to be in one piece, Marshall Byler."

Then she returned her attention to the harness. "This strap has given a lot of service and the leather is near worn through here and here." She indicated two places on the leather. "It could be fixed, but you might be better off with a new one."

"Let's see, if you aren't a Miller, you must be one of Rosemary's daughters. I've met two of your sisters." He eyed her. "You don't favor any of them, which is why I didn't make the connection. Why haven't I seen you at any of the singings?"

"Mended or made new?" she asked. "What will it be?"

Marshall drew himself up to his full height, bringing his eyes level with those intriguing green ones. "What's your name?"

Her lips tightened again, and flecks of gold tumbled in the green irises. "Lovage. Lovage Stutzman."

He rapped his knuckles on the counter. "Ah, I knew you were one of Rosemary's daughters. She was a Stutzman before she married Benjamin, right? My grandmother is distantly related to some New York Stutzmans. What kind of name is Lovage? I never knew an Amish girl called *Lovage*."

She tied a yellow paper tag to one end of his harness strap. "My mother likes herbs," she explained. "I'm Hannah Lovage, but I've never used Hannah."

He removed his straw hat and used his handkerchief to wipe his forehead. It had seemed so much cooler in the harness shop than outside, but it was definitely heating up inside. "Rosemary's eldest daughter, then. I know your stepbrother Will. You're the one who stayed behind to see to the sale of your mother's property."

She nodded, inspecting him through dark, thick lashes.

What was it about those eyes? And now that he studied her close up, something was striking about her high cheekbones, the curve of her jawline, the way her soft brown hair framed her face. *Ne*, perhaps she wasn't pretty by conventional standards, but she was handsome. She was what his grandmother would call a timeless beauty. A woman who would keep her looks over the years.

"And you live here now, right?" he asked. "Your stepbrother Will said everything was settled for your mother in upstate New York. He called you Lovey."

"Just moved in. Have you made a decision about the strap?" She held it in the flat of her palm.

"What?" He'd been concentrating so much on her appearance that he hadn't really heard what she'd said.

"Mended or replaced with new? Your *britchen* strap." She raised her eyebrows. "The reason you came to my stepfather's harness shop?"

"Um…whatever you think." He pressed his hands on the counter, leaning closer to her, and on impulse asked, "Lovey, would you let me drive you home from the singing this Friday night? It's going to be at Asa King's."

"It's Lovage and I would not." She wrote his name on the tag in small, perfect print. "Come back in five business days and this will be ready." She wrote on a receipt pad on the counter and ripped off the page.

"Why won't you let me take you home from the singing? Have you got a steady beau?"

"*Ne*, I don't have a beau. I won't go home with you from the singing because there is no singing at the Kings. It was canceled."

He grinned. "Fair enough." He thought fast, unwilling to walk away without some commitment from her. "Wait, there's a softball game Saturday night. At the bishop's farm. How about that? Men against the women. You do play, don't you? You look like a pitcher."

"Catcher," she replied. She handed him the receipt.

"So…is that a maybe you'll let me take you home Saturday night?"

She smiled sweetly. "*Ne*. It is not. Thank you for your business, Marshall Byler. Now if you'll excuse me, I'll take this back to the workroom."

"Will you at least think about riding home with me?" he called after her as she walked away.

She didn't respond, but Marshall wasn't in the least bit discouraged. She'd come around. He knew she would. The girls always did. "Nice meeting you, Lovey Stutzman. See you Saturday." He rapped his knuckles on the wooden counter a final time.

"Lovage," she called over her shoulder.

Marshall was still grinning when he walked out of the harness shop and back to the wagon, where Sam waited for him.

"What are you so happy about?" Sam asked, looking up at his big brother.

"I'm more than happy. I'm ecstatic, blissful, elated." Marshall climbed up into the wagon and took the reins. "Because I've just met the woman I'm going to marry."

In the workroom in the rear of Benjamin's harness shop, Lovage stopped beside the worktable where one of her sisters was using an oversize treadle sewing machine to stitch a strap on a new halter. Ginger, twenty-three, was two years younger than Lovage and twin to Bay Laurel.

Ginger paused, glanced up at her and offered a teasing smile. "I see you met Marshall Byler."

Lovage dropped the *britchen* strap on the long plank table. "It can be fixed, but you might be better off just making him a new one. Look at it and see what you think."

Preferring harness-making to housework and minding children, Ginger had worked in

Benjamin's shop for the past three years, first in New York where they used to live and now in Hickory Grove. Her small hands were deft at fashioning leather into everything from bridles to belts to dog leashes. Ginger may have been a woman, but she'd quickly become Benjamin's most skilled leather worker, surpassing even his sons.

"He's cute, isn't he?" Ginger's green eyes twinkled mischievously. "If I'd known that was him ringing the bell, I'd have waited on him myself."

"You know him?"

"Every Amish girl of marrying age in the county knows Marshall Byler. Wishes he'd ask her out."

"You, too?" Lovage asked, looking down at Ginger, who was seated on a wooden stool.

Ginger lowered her gaze to her work at hand. She lifted the foot of the sewing machine, adjusted the leather and dropped the foot again. "Are you going to let him take you home after the softball game?"

Lovage gazed at her sister.

Ginger was the prettiest of the Stutzman girls, blonde and green-eyed. And she was a flirt if there ever was such a thing among Old Order Amish. Back in New York, several mothers and a matchmaker had contacted their mother inquiring as to Ginger's availability as a possible match for their sons. Apparently, half the young men in Cattaraugus County, New York, were smitten with her. Rosemary had declared her second daughter too young to marry yet and had then whisked her off to Delaware.

"You were eavesdropping on my conversation with Marshall Byler?" Lovage asked, not even a little bit surprised.

"Maybe." Ginger nibbled on her lower lip. "From this stool, I hear all sorts of things in the front shop. Last week I heard that Mary Aaron Troyer is trying to match her twin boys with twin sisters from Kentucky." She shrugged. "Not sure they're keen on the idea. Are you going to the softball game?"

"You're certainly interested in my comings and goings." Lovage crossed her arms over her chest, pretending to be put out with the whole discussion. The truth was she was flattered by Marshall's attention. Though she didn't quite understand it. Not many boys expressed interest in her. She wasn't pretty enough or flirty enough. If a boy wanted to walk out with a Stutzman girl, Ginger was his choice every time. "And no one invited me."

Ginger ran the length of stitch and when the sewing machine was quiet again, she said, "It sounded to me as if Marshall Byler just invited you. Everyone's invited, anyway. It's a neighborhood game. We've gone before. Sometimes boys from Rose Valley even come." She snipped off a bit of loose thread from the halter with a pair of homemade scissors. "We play at Bishop Simon's house. He has a good field, even a backstop. He's nice. Jolly. And not too long-winded on Sundays. You'll love his wife, Annie. She'll make chocolate whoopie pies with peanut butter filling for the snack table. Wait until you taste them." Ginger took a breath and went on without waiting for Lovage to respond. "You should accept Marshall's offer."

"I certainly should not." Now Lovage was slightly peeved with her favorite sister for listening to what should have been a private conversation. Or maybe embarrassed. "I don't even know him—don't care to."

"Then you wouldn't mind if I ride home with him." Ginger tilted her head and giggled. "Will you?"

"You're impossible." Lovage tried to sound vexed, but it was all she could do not to laugh at her sister's boldness. She knew she should admonish Ginger for eavesdropping, but with four sisters, and now a houseful of brothers, who could expect privacy? It was impossible. And she could never be cross with one of her sisters for long. Certainly not over a boy. "You like all the single young men," she reminded her.

"Most, but not all," Ginger agreed. "Nothing wrong with liking the boys, so long as I remember everything Mam taught me about protecting my reputation." Her sister's amusement brought out her dimples. "I think Marshall is fun. Bay does, too. I know *she'd* ride home with him if he asked."

"He thinks he's so good-looking. Charming." Lovage frowned, secretly wondering if she dared be so bold as to accept Marshall's invitation. Then she asked herself, what would be the point? She wasn't the kind of girl a boy like him would be interested in. She couldn't fathom why he'd asked to take her home from the softball game. Was it a way to get in good with Ginger? But that made no sense, because Ginger already said she was interested in him. Marshall Byler probably knew he could get any girl in the country into his buggy.

"Marshall *is* good-looking. But also faithful." Ginger carefully studied the halter she'd finished, found no flaws and set it aside. She looked up at her sister. "And you really *aren't* interested in him?"

"*Ne*, I am not." Lovage said it with more conviction than she felt. "I just arrived in Hickory Grove. I'm certainly not going to get involved with some fast-talking farmer my first week here. Especially not now when Mam needs my help more than ever."

Ginger rolled the remaining thread onto the spool and tucked it into the drawer under the tabletop. "Probably just as well." She wrinkled her nose. "Marshall's not your type."

"And who is my type?" Lovage rested on hand on her hip. "Ishmael Slabaugh?" she asked, referring to the young man she'd come close to becoming betrothed to.

Her sister shook her head so hard that her scarf slipped off the back of her head. "*Ne*, I didn't care for him. Too serious. I'm glad you didn't marry him. You can do better." She removed the navy scarf and tied it over her hair again. Unruly tendrils of curly yellow hair framed her heart-shaped face, a face with a complexion like fresh cream, an unusually pretty face with practically no freckles and soft, dark brows that arched over thick lashes and large, intelligent eyes.

Envy was a sin, and only a wicked girl would be envious of a much-loved sister. But not resenting Ginger's golden hair, rosebud lips and pert nose wasn't easy when you were a brown-haired string bean with a too-full mouth and a firm German chin. Lovage had to remind herself to put it all into proper perspective. She, Ginger, Bay, Tara and Nettie had always been close, and having sisters that everyone called the catch of the county was her burden to bear. Aunt Jane, her *dat*'s older sister, hadn't made it any easier, always pointing out that Lovage took after her plain, sensible father and not her mother with her pretty face and quirky ways.

"It's probably just as well you don't ride home with Marshall. You're not suited for someone like him," Ginger continued. "He's looking for a fun girlfriend."

"What? And I'm not fun?" Lovage frowned, opening her arms wide. "How can you say that? I'm *fun*. I like to do fun things."

Ginger giggled. "You are a lot of things, but fun isn't the first thing that comes to mind when I think of you. You're strong and brave and caring. And you're dependable. You've always been there for your family and anyone in need. But *fun*?" She wrinkled her nose. "Not so much."

Lovage rolled her eyes.

"If anything," Ginger went on, "you can be the opposite of fun. You never do anything that's not comfortable for you. You never…

What's the Englisher phrase? Step out of your box? Bay and I are sure you'd have a better chance of finding a beau if you didn't take yourself and life so seriously."

"You're wrong," Lovage insisted. "I don't have a beau because I don't want one. And I certainly don't want a husband. Not right now, at least."

"Me, neither," Ginger confided. She rose from her seat and carried the newly finished halter to a peg on the wall. "I want to go to frolics and enjoy myself for a few years. When I marry, it will be for life. Plenty of time to be serious then."

"Mam thinks I should be looking for a husband," Lovage mused. "Just last night when we were getting ready for bed, she reminded me that I have a birthday coming up."

"You've got time. Twenty-five isn't old age." Ginger stood and perched on the edge of the worktable, crossing her legs at the knee and swinging a slim, bare foot. "And the sooner you marry, the sooner Mam will start thinking it's time for Bay and me to make a match. And, like I told you, neither of us is in a hurry."

"*Goot*. We agree on something."

"But…" Ginger chuckled and shook her head. "Since you brought up the subject, I may as well have my say as chew on it like an old cow's cud."

"Say it then," Lovage replied. "You know you will, anyway."

"Okay, so maybe…" Ginger leaned forward and looked her straight in the eye. "Maybe you shouldn't be so stubborn, and listen to someone once in a while. You know I love you more than gingerbread, and I only want what's best for you."

Lovage grimaced. "All right, all right. Say it and get it over with."

"I've been talking to Bay and we agree. Our advice to you as the new girl is to make friends and go to the singings and the ball games and the frolics. Enjoy yourself before you settle down with a husband and babies. I'm going to the softball game. I think we all are. You should come with us. You're a mean catcher, and we need one. Most of the girls are afraid of the ball."

Lovage suddenly felt nervous. "What if this Marshall pesters me to ride home with him?"

Ginger shrugged. "I doubt he will." She broke into a sassy grin. "Not when I give him my best smile."

Lovage sighed and glanced away. A part of her wanted to go to the softball game, but this thing with Marshall suddenly seemed like so much pressure. "But what if he does?"

"Then you should go ride home with him. Like I said, you're not his type, but it might be a good way to meet other boys. To be friendly with Marshall. He knows everyone in the county."

Lovage crossed her arms over her chest. A part of her wanted to tell Marshall she'd ride home with him, just to prove to Ginger that she could be fun.

"Come on. I dare you to do it." Still grinning, Ginger poked Lovage in the arm with her finger. "Tell you what, sister. If you ride home from the softball game with Marshall Byler Saturday night, I'll take your turn at washing dishes for a whole week."

Chapter Two

Lovage knelt on a carpet of thick moss and pulled up a few dandelions that were sprouting up beside the fish pond. "Your herb beds are coming along beautifully, Mam. I didn't think you'd be this far along with them." She dropped the dandelions into a bucket with the few weeds she'd already pulled. "And the waterfall is perfect for this spot. I love the sound of the water. It's so relaxing."

Her mother placed freshly cut sprigs of lavender in a basket and rested her large, dirt-streaked hands on her hips. "I'm so glad you're finally here, Lovey. I've missed you so much. No one appreciates my garden like you do." She studied the twenty-foot, oblong pond with its bubbling cascade, miniature lily pads, cattails and decorative rock border, and smiled. "I wish I could take credit for this, but I can't. The pond, the Irish moss and the wrought-iron bench were already here when Benjamin brought me to look at the farm. When I walked through that gate and saw this herb garden and the flowing water, I fell in love with the place. I told him that this was the one before I even set foot in the house."

Lovage stood up and brushed the soil off her apron. She was barefoot, as was her mother, and both wore midcalf-length dresses, oversize aprons with large pockets and wide-brimmed straw bonnets over their prayer *kapps*.

Lovage was pleased that she and her mother had found a few minutes to be alone, even if it was to work in the garden. As the firstborn, she and her *mam* had always been close, and had become more so after her mother had been widowed three years ago. Lovage had missed her mother dearly in the time they'd been apart. She'd always considered her mother her best friend, so this morning was doubly precious.

When her mother married their late father's best friend the previous year, Lovage had remained behind in New York when her *mam* and her new husband, Benjamin, and all their children, had made the move to Delaware. Lovage had four sisters and a brother, and Benjamin had five sons still at home, so it had been quite an effort to move them all. While the family got settled in Delaware, their mother had entrusted her with the responsibility of selling the livestock and the farm equipment, as well as disposing of the household goods.

Blending two large families and two homes into one wasn't done easily or quickly, and the couple had decided that a new start, a new home and a new community would give them the greatest opportunity for success. Lovage was glad to remain behind to help her mother in whatever way she could, but she'd missed the bustle of her large family and was glad when the last of the decisions were made, the final shipment of household goods was on its way to Delaware, and she was free to come.

"Smell this lavender," her mother said, bringing her back into the present. "And see how the thyme is growing. I was afraid that it wouldn't. But there's more rainfall here than back home, and the pond helps. There's a good market for dried lavender, for sachets and hanging arrangements."

"The soil seems free of rocks," Lovage observed.

Her mother laughed. "No rocks in Delaware. At least not down here. Benjamin says it gets a little rocky upstate near the Pennsylvania state line. This whole garden used to be fenced in for the dairy cows. I wouldn't be surprised if my hoe took root and blossomed."

"The cows had a pond and wrought-iron bench? I'm confused."

"For years it was a cow pasture and then, when the English farmer retired, his wife wanted a pretty pond and an herb and flower garden. You can see someone loved and tended it. Either that or the cows wanted somewhere nice to sit."

Lovage laughed, picturing a cow sitting on the iron bench with a gardening trowel between her hooves. "I can see that this is a wonderful spot for you. But you inherited Grossmama's green thumb. Any plant will grow for you."

"And you have the gift, too," her *mam* replied. "It's a true blessing."

Lovage clasped both of her mother's strong hands and led her to the wide iron bench with the high back and the grapevine pattern. A grape arbor arched overhead with spreading leaves and tiny green concord grapes, providing relief from the hot July sun, something they both could relish. "Sit with me," she urged. "You've been on your feet since before six this morning."

Her mother's smile lit her green eyes. "And that's different from every other morning in what way, *dochtah*?"

"It isn't. That's the thing. You shouldn't have to get up so early. You have Ginger and Bay and the younger girls to help you with breakfast and the chores. And now me. I want you to take better care of yourself."

"It's a wonder how I managed before you got here, my love."

"Be serious." She caught her mother's hand again and clasped it with affection, taking in the broken fingernails and calluses. *The apple doesn't fall far from the tree*, Lovage thought with a glance at her own hands. Too bad she didn't inherit Mam's sunny disposition and lovely features instead of taking after her father.

She looked into her mother's smiling face and tried to reason with her. "You have to let us help you, especially now with all these extra boys in the house. Boys needing clothes washed, eating everything that isn't tacked down, tracking in mud and wood shavings. And now that I'm here, I'll be able to take over a lot of your chores, just like at home in New York."

"This is our home now." Her mother pulled her hand free and hugged her. "And those *boys* are Benjamin's sons and now my sons and your stepbrothers."

"I know that."

Her *mam* patted her cheek fondly. "Of course, I know how much you did for me both before my marriage to Benjamin and after. But...now that you're here, things have to be different. It's time you started thinking about yourself. About the life you'll have separate from me—marriage, your own home, babies, God willing."

"I told you I don't want to talk about that." Lovage gazed out over the garden. "My place right now is with you, helping you."

"Oh, Lovage." Her mother sighed. "You being my eldest, it's natural that you feel the most responsible. But it's time you flew the coop, my chick. Find yourself a good man and let him court you the way you deserve."

Against her will, Lovage thought of Marshall Byler and how he had flirted with her the previous day at the harness shop. "And what if that's not what I want?"

Her mother drew back, looking at her with true concern. "You don't want to marry and have your own home? You don't want a husband and children? I don't believe that. Children are God's greatest blessings. And His grace, of course. If any woman was born to be a mother, it's you, Lovage."

Lovage removed her straw hat and dropped it onto the brick walkway, letting the breeze ruffle her hair. Carefully thinking over her words before they spilled out all higgledy-piggledy, she straightened her starched white *kapp* and repinned the back of her hair securely. "I do want those things. It's every girl's dream… Her own kitchen…red-cheeked babies with sticky hands and butter-fly kisses. But—"

"But nothing. If you want those things, you need a husband. And you need a part-ner to share the burdens of life," her mother said softly. "A godly man who shares your faith, and will laugh with you and lend you his strength when you most need it. Don't you want that?"

"I do want all those things someday," Lovage assured her. "But not now. Now, I want only to be here with you, to help you through this."

"Help me *through this*?" Her mother's eyes widened in puzzlement and then she sighed. "Lovey—"

"There you are, my Rosebud," boomed a deep male voice. Benjamin was a sturdy, fiftyish man of medium height, with rusty brown hair streaked with gray and a pleasant, weathered face with a high forehead and a broad nose under his straw hat. His full beard had a reddish cast and that, too, had begun to gray. At the moment, he was carrying a tray of assorted herb seedlings and had a twenty-pound bag of bonemeal tucked under one arm.

"I should have known to look here first." He swung the white picket gate wide and strode into the garden. "And you with her, *dochtah*. What do you think of the place? I warn you, your mother had the final say. So if it doesn't please you…" He chuckled. "You must blame her."

Lovage's mother laughed with him.

"Speak up, wife," he implored. "Where do you want the bonemeal?"

She got up and went to him. "Anywhere at all, Benjamin," she answered, taking the tray of seedlings from him.

"That's no answer. Shall I drop it in the pond or balance it on a fence post?"

"Anywhere will do, but preferably not in the water," Rosemary said, setting the plants on the ground. "Here."

"She's full of honey-do's, this wife of mine." Benjamin winked at Lovage conspiratorially and lowered the bag of bonemeal to the ground beside a section of newly worked, bare dirt. "You see how she treats me?" He straightened and slipped an arm around her mother's waist.

"Go on with you." Her *mam* blushed like a schoolgirl. "You're embarrassing Lovage. What will she think of us?"

"That we suit each other like bread and honey," he teased, wrapping his other arm around his wife.

Giggling, Rosemary tried to push her husband's hands away, but with no great effort.

Uncomfortable, Lovage glanced away. She truly liked her stepfather, but their outrageous behavior was going to take some getting used to. She could never remember her father acting so, and she knew their marriage had been a happy one. Physical affection wasn't something one saw often with an Amish couple. And certainly not one of their age. Both were old enough to be grandparents and Benjamin soon would be. His married daughter, Mary, was expecting twins.

"See, what did I tell you? Behave yourself in front of the children." Still chuckling, her mother stepped out of her husband's embrace. "Go see to your harnesses and buggy wheels and leave us in peace."

"There now, wife, I meant no harm," Benjamin said. "And no disrespect to either of you," he added, looking to Lovage.

"I know that." Lovage nodded, but avoided his gaze.

It was true. In spite of the current situation, she was pleased that her mother had found someone who obviously adored her and could provide for her. It was only natural that mixing two large families into one would require adjustment. Her aunt Paula thought her sister Rosemary had lost her mind to accept the offer of a man with six children, five under his roof.

"You must have chores of your own to do," her mother told Benjamin.

"If you say so, Rosebud," he agreed. "Unless you need me here."

She smiled at him. "I do not. Now off with you, before you embarrass poor Lovage even more." She watched him trudge away with a feigned sad expression. When the gate shut behind him, she turned to her daughter. "You mustn't pay his silliness any mind. Benjamin is so pleased to have you with us. And you're going to like it here," she added.

Lovage nodded.

Leaving the home where she'd been born and grown up hadn't been as difficult as Lovage had thought it might be. She could see that the move to a new place and a new, larger home that neither her mother nor Benjamin had shared with another spouse seemed the wisest course. It was too soon to know if she would like Delaware, but her mother clearly did. And Lovage was happy to be reunited with her sisters and mother, and her little brother.

"It seems like a good house and community," she said. "Of course, I haven't met the new bishop and preachers yet. Or the other families."

"You will like them very well," her mother said. "The sermons are short and pithy and our church members welcoming. Everyone has embraced us and they're eager to meet you.

"Now, to get back to what we were talking about before we were interrupted," her mother continued. "Why is it that you have set your mind against being courted by a suitable young man now? A sweet and capable girl like you. You could have your pick if you'd just—"

"Mam, please. Don't talk like that." She felt her cheeks grow warm. She knew what she was. Too tall, too lanky...too opinionated. But that wasn't the point. "It's not about me.

It's about you. A woman your age…in your *condition*," she intoned.

"In my *condition*?" The amusement seeped from her mother's face and her chin firmed. "I am neither sick nor so decrepit that I can't run my own household. I'm forty-five and carrying a child. It is not an illness. It's a natural condition for a married woman and it's a blessing. God has given Benjamin and me another life to cherish."

Lovage knew she blushed. To have such a conversation with her mother made her uncomfortable, but if she was determined to have it, have it they would. "A pregnancy at your age is considered high risk. I'm worried about you and it's my duty to help you through this."

"Goose feathers! I'm as strong as a horse." Chuckling, she picked up the basket she'd been using to gather herbs. "You're the one who needs help, Lovage. And I would be neglecting my duty as your mother if I didn't see you happily wed to a good man. I think you should take that young man's offer and ride home with him from the softball game."

Lovage whipped around to look at her mother. "Ginger should not have told you. He wasn't—" She knew her cheeks were burning bright. "He didn't— Ginger should mind her own business."

Her mother headed for the garden gate. "It wasn't Ginger. It was Bay who—"

"How did Bay know Marshall asked me to ride home with him?" She crossed her arms obstinately. "I'm not going to, of course."

Her mother raised her brows under her broad-brimmed hat. "Marshall, is it? Your stepbrother Will's friend? Nice-looking young man." She made a clicking sound between her teeth. "And from a good family. I've met his grandmother, Lynita. Faithful woman. Knows how to work hard and live with joy." She opened the gate. "A good choice for a suitor, Lovey."

"He's *not* my suitor," Lovage called as the gate swung shut, leaving her alone in the garden.

The following morning, Lovage made her way back to the garden, hoping to beat the full heat of the day. Her mother was letting out the seams on one of her dresses, and the younger girls had taken over the task of cleaning up the kitchen and starting the chicken and dumplings for the midday meal. Lovage had offered to plant the new seedlings Benjamin had bought, and to finish weeding around the fish pond.

Family breakfast had been as noisy and satisfying as Lovage remembered. She approved of her mother's new house, especially the large kitchen with its attached, open dining room. Benjamin's twenty-two-year-old twins, Jacob and Joshua, who were apprenticed to a cabinetmaker, had built a fourteen-foot oak trestle table. The table provided enough room for all of them to eat together and this morning her brother, Jesse, who was ten, had declared it the finest dining table he'd ever eaten at.

How she'd missed Jesse's mischievous face in the months they'd been apart. He was brown-haired like her and her father, with green eyes, and his own special lopsided grin. That morning, Benjamin had promised to take Jesse to look at a pony for sale and the boy was so excited he could hardly sit still for grace, let alone eat his bacon and eggs. It was clear to Lovage that Jesse was very fond of his stepfather, and soon would begin to think of him as simply his *dat*. It made Lovage sad to think that eventually her little brother would barely remember their own father. She knew it was best for Jesse; it was just hard, no matter how much she liked Benjamin. But as her aunt Jane said, "Life moves on for the living. My brother is in heaven and beyond those earthly cares. You can't stop change. You may as well embrace it."

Lovage gazed out over the garden. It had rained sometime in the night, and the soil was wet. The garden smelled deliciously of mint, sage and rosemary. Finding her rhythm in planting, Lovage soon discarded the digging trowel and used her fingers. She hiked up her skirt to keep the worst of the mud off it and knelt on a folded-up burlap bag as she carefully transplanted each basil and tarragon seedling.

Herbs preferred cool weather, so July wasn't the best time to put them in the ground, but Benjamin probably hadn't realized that when he'd bought up the remainder of the neighbor's greenhouse herb stock. Her mother wouldn't have wanted to discourage him by rejecting his gift, so Lovage was determined to do her best to save the seedlings.

On her hands and knees, with her skirt hiked up, she planted most of the tray. Then, when she had to stretch to reach the last of the open area in the bed, she reached too far and slipped on the wet topsoil. She went down on both elbows, throwing dirt onto the bodice and sleeves of her dress, as well as liberally covering both arms, elbow to wrist, with wet soil. *"Atch!"* she exclaimed, and spat the dirt from between her lips.

"You okay?" came a male voice from behind her.

Lovage froze, not knowing who the voice belonged to, though it seemed familiar. Then, realizing what she must look like, sprawled in the herb bed, covered in mud, she scrambled to rise. *"Ya,"* she called, "I'm fine. I…" In her effort to get up, she succeeded only in slipping again and falling forward into the dirt again. "Oh!" As she went down, her right hand flattened a small seedling, while her elbow took out two more. That was when a pair of strong male hands closed around her shoulders and lifted her to her feet.

"You sure you're all right?" he asked.

She whirled around. Mortified, cheeks scalding, she raised her gaze to look directly into Marshall Byler's amused eyes. "Oh," she breathed.

"Oh," he said, managing, somehow, to make it sound flirty.

"What…what are you doing here?" she sputtered, taking a step back from him. Out of his arms. She glanced down at her dress and bare feet covered in dirt, and then back at him as she shoved her skirt down where it had gotten tangled in her apron. Which was now also muddy.

He grinned and offered her a big blue handkerchief from his pocket. "You've got mud on your forehead," he informed her. "Right here." He tapped his own forehead in the center. "I can get it for you if you—"

"You'll do no such thing." She snatched the handkerchief from him and dabbed at her forehead.

"And…and your nose," he said helpfully, pointing.

Lovage rubbed her nose furiously with the blue fabric.

He tipped the broad brim of his straw hat as if to get a better look at her. "To answer your question, I came to check on my harness. One of your sisters sent me out here to ask you. Bay, I think?"

Lovage huffed. "I told you it would be five business days. Bay could have—" She suddenly realized that Bay had sent him out to the garden on purpose. Ginger was probably in on it. And their mother, as well, for all she knew. She blushed even harder and went back to scrubbing her nose with his handkerchief. "Bay shouldn't have sent you out here. She could have looked up the work order. You only dropped it off two days ago."

"A good thing for you she did send me, because I don't think you would have managed to get up anytime today." He grinned, indicating the wet spot in the garden. "Not the way you were slipping and sliding in that mud." Then he laughed, the sound deep and infectious.

Lovage didn't want to laugh. She knew that if she did, he'd take it as encouragement and continue his flirty talk. But she couldn't help it. She looked down at her arms and dress again and began to laugh, sounding not like herself, but oddly enough, more like Ginger. "I think I would have managed," she said, when she could talk again. "I'd have made it to my feet by noon."

His blue eyes danced. "Suppertime at the latest."

Still chuckling, she walked over to the pond, knelt and washed the worst of the mud off her arms. Next, she dipped her feet in, one at a time. Marshall watched as she wiped her wet hands on a relatively clean place on her apron. "Better?" she asked.

"Somewhat," he conceded.

"Goot." She met his gaze and it took her a moment to break free of it. "But you've made the trip for nothing." She shrugged. "I told

you the harness wouldn't be done for at least five business days."

"Ne." He held up one finger. "I remember exactly what your words were. You told me to come back in five days. You didn't say the harness wouldn't be done today."

"But it isn't."

He made a show of appearing sad, thrusting his lower lip out in a pout. "A pity. I need it."

"If I could have fixed it for you, I would have, but it isn't what I do. Ginger and my stepbrothers, they're the harness workers. Benjamin has other work orders, people who came before you. They need their harnesses and halters and bridles, too. It wouldn't be fair to fix yours out of turn."

Lovage glanced back at the muddy mess of an herb bed. She'd have to salvage as many of the plants as she could. But she wasn't about to attempt it with Marshall as a witness. She turned away and walked down the path toward the gate, hoping he would follow. Hoping he would leave.

"So…what you're telling me is that *you* can't fix my *britchen* strap?" he asked, following her. "Only your sister can."

"I can't use the sewing machine. It takes a

knack. Otherwise, you just break the thread. And sometimes the needle."

"Pity," he said, walking two steps behind her. "You'll be in over your head when we marry if you can't sew."

She stopped short, whirled around and looked at him. "What did you just say?"

"I said, if you can't sew, it could be a problem. I've never known an Amish woman who couldn't sew." He knitted his brows. "How will you make shirts for me or baby clouts?"

"*Baby clouts?* Who's making *baby clouts*?" She looked up at him wide-eyed, wondering if the summer heat had gotten to his head. Except that it was still morning and not all that hot out. "I was talking about harness-making. My sister is apprenticing as a harness maker. I can *sew*. I don't sew *leather*." She caught her breath, flustered again. "And that's not what I meant. You're putting words in my mouth." She dropped her hands to her hips. "What did you say about me being in over my head?"

His smile widened. "I said you'd be in over your head when we marry if—"

"What are you talking about, marry?" she interrupted. "I don't know you. We're not even—" She blushed again. "We're not even walking out together."

"You're absolutely right," he said, interrupting her. "And that's a problem. We're not walking out yet." He sidestepped around her and opened the gate, standing back and holding it for her. "And I think that's important to our relationship. We should get to know each other before we take our vows. It's the custom here in Kent County. We walk out together, court, marry. In that order." He winked at her. "Is it different where you come from?"

"Enough." She raised her hands, palms out. "I'm not amused by you. We aren't walking out together. We aren't courting. And we certainly aren't getting married. You came to get a harness mended. I waited on you. That's it. That's the only connection we have."

"Not exactly." In an exaggerated motion with his hand, he indicated the garden behind them. "We've had this time together."

"What are you talking about now?" she asked, still flustered, wishing desperately that she wasn't. She also wished he wasn't so handsome. That his forearms weren't so tanned and muscular. That his smile wasn't so…beautiful.

"And we're neighbors," he told her. "We have that connection."

"We are *not* neighbors. You live two miles away."

His grin widened to crinkle his entire face.

Marshall had a high forehead and a dimple in the center of his square chin. With his broad shoulders and self-assured manner, he was one of the most attractive young men she'd ever met. Which made her nervous. She wasn't used to attention from such a cute guy and she half suspected that he was poking fun at her. Because surely he wasn't *really* interested in her.

Once, at a frolic when she was fifteen, a cute boy had caught her eye and she'd wanted him to notice her. She'd even broken her own rule and smiled at him, trying to flirt casually like Ginger did. It worked. The boy had noticed her, all right, but he'd only turned to a friend and whispered something she couldn't quite make out. She had heard the word *broomstick*, then they'd both laughed, obviously at her. She'd cried into her pillow half the night, and she still remembered the slight painfully. Not for all the apples in an orchard would she make the same mistake a second time.

"Ah," Marshall continued, holding up his finger to her again. "You asked someone about me. You wanted to know where I lived, which means you *are* interested in me." He pointed at her. "Admit it. You like me."

"I do not *like* you," she protested.

"You don't like me?" He opened his arms. "What have I done to deserve that? I'm a nice fellow. Ask anyone. They'll tell you. Your brother Will likes me. He and I have become good friends."

"Will is my stepbrother," she corrected.

Marshall removed his straw hat and pushed back his dark hair. It was nice hair, neatly trimmed and thick. "That's what he said when I asked him about you last night."

He smiled at her and she felt her pulse quicken. He *did* have a sweet smile, a dangerous smile that made her stumble over her words and confuse her thinking.

Marshall met her gaze. "I wanted to see you again," he said softly. "That's why I came to check on my harness. I was hoping to see you, Lovey."

Suddenly, the oxygen was sucked out of the air. The sound of her pet name on his lips made her throat tighten. But she liked it. She did. Marshall was teasing her again, wasn't he? A boy like him couldn't like a girl like her.

Could he?

"I wanted to see you and ask if you're coming to the softball game tomorrow night," he went on.

"Maybe," she said quickly, still flustered.

He just kept *looking* at her. "I... I haven't decided yet."

"I see." Marshall nodded. "Well, I hope you do. And if you do, will you let me drive you home in my buggy? It's a nice buggy..."

It had been a long time since anyone had asked Lovage to ride home in a buggy with him. So long that she didn't know how to respond. Lovage bit down on her lower lip.

Then she heard the sound of feminine giggling. She and Marshall both glanced in the direction of a hedge of blueberry bushes and she spotted her sisters Bay, Tara and Nettie all peeking around the hedge, watching them.

Lovage quickly looked back at Marshall. He was waiting, smiling. He didn't give a lick that they had an audience.

"Come on, Lovey." He reached out and touched her elbow. "It'll be fun. Say you'll ride home with me Saturday night."

She swallowed hard and grasped at the first answer that came to mind. "I might," she told him. "If you're on your best behavior."

"I'll take that as a yes." Marshall walked past her, his stride long and powerful. "It's a date," he said, loudly enough not only for her sisters behind the blueberry bushes to hear, but possibly everyone up at the house.

"But, Marshall," she called after him. "I didn't say—"

"See you tomorrow, Lovey."

All Lovage heard then was a burst of giggles from the blueberry hedge.

Chapter Three

"You want to go ahead and get Toby un-harnessed?" Marshall asked his brother. The wagon had barely come to a halt in the barnyard and he pressed the reins into Sam's hands and leaped to the ground. "Rub him down before you let him into the pasture. It's a hot day."

"*Ya.*" Twelve-year-old Sam, a carbon copy of a younger Marshall, gripped the wide leather reins with both hands, seeming to puff up with pride at being given the task. "I'll give 'im a good rub and a scoop of grain."

"Mind you, the harness needs to be wiped down, as well." Marshall backed away from the wagon, clamping his hand down over his straw hat. Sounds coming from the henhouse distracted him for a moment. He could hear chickens squawking and flapping their wings.

He looked back to Sam. "Give me a holler if you need any help."

Sam eyed his big brother from under the brim of his hat, which was identical to Marshall's. Small for his age, he sometimes struggled with the chores requiring brute strength or simply height, but he more than made up for it with heart. And smarts. If he wasn't strong enough to do something, like lift a hundred-pound bag of feed, he'd throw together a contraption of one sort or the other to accomplish the task. He had pulleys and levers all over the barn, mechanisms he'd built himself from scraps he found around the farm or scavenged at the county dump or friends' trash cans.

"I got it," Sam said. He wasn't a talker. But he was a hard worker. He was the first one up in the morning, the last to go to bed, and that was only when Marshall or their *grossmammi* sent him up to his room—with the warning there would be no reading. Otherwise, Sam would be up half the night scouring books and magazines on Plain ways to make work go easier on their farm.

Marshall watched Sam ease the wagon toward the drive-through shed his little brother had designed himself. It was a clever lean-to attached to the main barn, just wide enough

for a horse and buggy to pull in to get out of
the rain or sun. There, the vehicle, the horse
and the man could stay out of the elements
while hitching or unhitching. And when it
was time to go somewhere, the horse could
be hitched to the front of the buggy or wagon
and then walk right out without having to
back up. Their bishop had liked the design so
much he'd built one himself at his own property, saying it would come in handy because
a man with his responsibilities had to travel
day or night, snow or rain.

The chickens continued to kick up a ruckus
and Marshall strode across the barnyard,
wondering if a fox had gotten in the henhouse. It had happened the previous year and
they had lost half their layers in one night.
But it was midday, nearly dinner, and not the
time of day a fox was usually up and about.

As he crossed the barnyard, Marshall
took in the big barn and multiple outbuildings. Every structure looked neat and tidy,
all painted a traditional red with white trim:
the old dairy barn, the henhouse, the smokehouse and carriage shed, the granary and
other assorted structures. The dirt driveway
was raked, the grass mowed and the beds
of flowers weeded. And off behind the neat,
white clapboard farmhouse, his garden of

raised beds, rather than the rows his father had always planted, were neatly weeded. The raised beds were new this year. It had taken Sam two planting seasons to convince Marshall to make the change, but Marshall had to admit it was a good one. They were yielding more crops in a smaller space with less effort.

The sight of his little Eden made Marshall smile. He and Sam had grown up here, Marshall with both his parents, Sam with only their *dat*, after their *mam* died giving birth to him. Then four years ago, their *dat* died of cancer, and at the age of twenty-six Marshall had become the head of the family, responsible for his grandmother and his little brother. The transition from being the eldest son to the man of the house had been difficult at first for Marshall, especially with the transition from big brother to parent to Sam. It had put an end to his *rumspringa* days and nights of courting the prettiest girls in the county. But the three of them, Marshall, Sam and Grossmammi, had worked through their sorrow and come out the other side, seeing the good in the life God had given them.

The volume of the disturbance in the henhouse became louder and Marshall ran the last couple steps and flung open the door, half expecting to meet a fox with one of his chickens it its mouth. Instead, he came face-to-face with his petite grandmother, holding a basket of eggs in one hand and a flapping chicken by the feet in the other.

"Got her," Grossmammi exclaimed, holding the chicken high in the air.

The chicken squawked and beat its wings, trying desperately to escape her grip. "Thought she'd get away with it, she did."

She thrust the chicken upward and Marshall took a step back, raising his hands to keep the chicken from flapping its wings in his face.

He laughed. "Grossmammi, what are you doing?"

She lowered the chicken to her side, letting its head brush the dirt floor of the henhouse, but still held tightly to it. "Collecting eggs."

He grinned at his grandmother, who stood five feet tall only when she wore her heavy-soled black shoes. Despite her short stature, she was a hearty-sized woman, round with chubby cheeks and a smile that was infectious. Several wisps of gray hair had come free from her elder's black prayer *kapp*, evidence of the struggle that had apparently taken place between her and the black-and-white-potted Dominique chicken.

"I mean, what are you doing with the chicken?" He pointed.

She held it up as if she was surprised to find it in her hand. "I warned Emily, if she pecked me again, into the stew pot she went. I should have known not to buy any more Dominicker chicks. Small brains." She lowered the chicken and looked at him. "She'll make us a nice supper tomorrow night."

He removed his hat and wiped his brow before returning it to his head. "And how does Emily feel about that?"

"She should have thought of that before she pecked my hand again." She held up the hand that held the basket of eggs. "Look, she drew blood."

He glanced at her hand, which was, indeed, bloody. "She peck you before or after you hung her upside down by her feet?" He suppressed a smile. It made his grandmother angry when she thought he was making fun of her. And an angry Lynita Byler he did not want to deal with today. He was in too good a mood.

"She drew blood, *sohn*," she said, shaking the chicken. It began to flap its wings again, but with less effort. "I can't have my own chickens pecking me!"

He smiled. Even though he was her *kins-*

kind, her grandchild, and not her son, it had been her habit for several years now to call him her own and that somehow eased his pain of being an orphan. Even being a grown man of thirty, he found it hard sometimes to be without parents. "I see your point." He studied the chicken for a moment. "But I'm afraid she's going to be awfully tough. How old is Emily? Three years old? Four?"

"Old enough to know not to peck the hand that feeds her grain," Grossmammi said indignantly.

He reached out and took the basket of eggs from her. "The other thing to take into consideration is that tomorrow is the softball game. Will says there's talk of cooking hamburgers and hot dogs. In that case, we won't be having supper at home. I know you don't want to miss a softball game and potluck to eat a tough old chicken."

She harrumphed, raised the bird high again and said, "Last time, Emily. I promise you that." Then she lowered the old hen to the ground and Emily had the good sense to hit the ground running.

Marshall stepped aside to let his grandmother pass and closed the henhouse door behind her.

"You go to Troyer's and get your *britchen*

strap repaired?" she asked, watching him latch the door securely.

They crossed the sunny barnyard side by side, Marshall shortening his stride so his grandmother could keep up. She was wearing a rose-colored dress today, her bare feet dirty from work in the garden that morning.

"I went to Miller's," he told her. "Will's stepfather's harness shop. Thought it would be neighborly to go there rather than Troyer's. Give them the business. Which is a good thing because I met the woman I'm going to marry," he told her.

She stopped and cocked her head. She wore tiny, wire-frame glasses with lenses that darkened in the sunlight. Marshall couldn't see her eyes now, but her tone of voice was enough of a reprimand.

"Your wife!" she exclaimed. "You've already courted and become betrothed? Banns going to be read on Sunday?" She started walking again and he was the one who had to keep up.

"Not moving quite that quickly, Mammi," he said, using her nickname. "What's the matter? I thought you'd be pleased."

"That you're ready to bring a wife into this house." She nodded. "I am. A man going to be thirty-one come Christmas Eve, you should have a wife and a house full of children. God willing," she added quickly. "Who are you talking about? One of Rosemary's girls, I suppose? That Ginger is a flirt. You've always been drawn to a pretty face."

"Not Ginger. Lovage. Rosemary's oldest. She's just come to Hickory Grove this week." They cut across the grass toward the back porch. "She's been in New York settling her mother's affairs this last year."

Lynita made a clicking sound between her teeth. "Lovage? What kind of a name is that?"

"Lovage is an herb," he explained to her as they rounded one of the hickory trees his grandfather, Lynita's husband, had planted two generations ago. They hadn't grown naturally on the property, but there were so many in the area, Marshall's father had told him, that Moses had dug up soldiers in the woods, planted them all around the house he built for his new wife. And now, though Grossdaddi had been dead two decades, they shaded the home where his sons and grandsons had been born and, God willing, his great-grandchildren would be born.

It was interesting to Marshall that in all his running-around years when he was in his early twenties, children had been the last thing on his mind. All he had wanted was a fast horse to pull his courting buggy and a pretty girl beside him. Marriage hadn't been a consideration and being a father had fallen even behind that. But the last few months, he'd begun to feel a need to settle down and have a family of his own. Maybe it was his grandmother nagging him, or maybe it was God directing, Marshall didn't know. What he *did* know was that Lovey Stutzman was the woman for him.

"I like Rosemary, but a bit of an odd duck, isn't she? And marrying at her age, to a man with all those boys? Brave she is, too." Lynita studied him through her dark glasses. "I'm glad you're thinking about finding a good woman, but I think you'd best stay closer to home. A girl born and raised here." She went up the porch steps.

He followed her. "Not this again, Mammi. Faith is a perfectly nice girl, but—"

"She can cook," his grandmother interrupted. "She can sew as fine a stitch on a quilt as I've ever seen, and you won't have to worry about her bringing any fancy ideas from New York. She grew up here in Hickory Grove just like you. She knows how things are done." At the top of the steps, she took the basket from him, an egg basket she'd woven herself. "I like her name better, too."

Marshall glanced away, grinning. His grandmother was persistent, if nothing else. She'd been touting their neighbor Faith King's qualities since Easter Sunday, when she and Faith's mother had talked after services and she had learned that Faith was ready to start looking for a serious suitor. Faith was young and pretty and she cooked as fine a stuffed pig's maw as he had ever eaten. He'd give her that, but she didn't light a spark in him. Not the way Lovey had.

He looked at his grandmother, who, standing on the porch with him still on the stairs, was nearly his height.

"Grossmammi, you know I respect your opinion, but—"

"And her father's land meets ours to the north. Couldn't be more convenient. Eldest girl and no sons to inherit." She lifted her snowy-white brows. "The two farms together would make a fine piece of land someday."

"As I was saying before you interrupted—"

"*Ne*, I didn't interrupt. I'm older than you are, and wiser." She pointed a tiny finger at him. "It's not an interruption coming from an elder. It's a fact."

He chuckled, shaking his head. "You're not marrying me off to Faith King, Mammi." He turned and went down the steps. First, he was going to check on Sam's progress unhitching Toby, and then he intended to work on replacing a rotting post in the grape arbor until his grandmother called them for dinner. "I appreciate your concern, but I'll find my own wife." At the bottom of the steps, he turned to her, opening his arms wide. "I already have."

Lovage walked off the softball field, carrying a catcher's mask under her arm. The community softball games were so popular in Hickory Grove that Bishop Simon not only had a ballfield on his property, but equipment: bats, balls, extra gloves and an old catcher's mask he'd found at Spence's Bazaar. Lovage hadn't been to the market in nearby Dover, where Amish and Englishers sold wares and foodstuffs and shopped, but she'd heard it mentioned multiple times since her arrival in Delaware. It was a place one could find not just treasures like a used catcher's mask, but also handmade items like quilts and wooden crafts, deli sandwiches, homemade cakes and doughnuts and pickles and preserves.

"Nice game," one of the young men, John Mary Byler, who had played third base on her team, said as he walked by. He was with Lovage's stepbrothers Jacob and Joshua, who were identical twins. With matching haircuts, even knowing them her whole life, Lovage had to listen to their speech patterns to identify which was Jacob and which was Joshua. Their eldest brother, Ethan, said they purposely tried to do things exactly the same way, copying each other's gestures and such to confuse people purposely for fun.

Lovage nodded and looked down at the ground, feeling self-conscious. John Mary hadn't wanted her on his team; it had been obvious from the look on his face when Bishop Simon had divvied them up. She supposed this was his way of apologizing, now that he knew she could play softball pretty well, but he still made her feel uncomfortable. Or maybe it was his cousin Marshall Byler who was making her nervous. Marshall had played for the other team, but had kept up a running dialogue with her the whole afternoon, complimenting her on every good throw she made from behind the plate and assuring her she'd get the next one if she missed a strike thrown to her. He was the pitcher for the other team. And now the game was over and families were packing up to go home to tuck little ones into bed. Young men and women of courting age were beginning to break into groups or even pairs to spend an hour together—chaperoned, of course—before they went home.

"Thirsty?" Marshall seemed to come out of nowhere to walk beside her across the grass toward the area where families were packing up the leftovers from the cookout potluck. In the distance, she could see her mother filling one of their three picnic baskets while speaking to Jesse. Benjamin was shamelessly putting covers on food dishes and handing them to her as if every fifty-year-old Amish man cleaned up after supper.

"I'm sorry. What?" Lovage glanced at Marshall. They were the same height, something she hadn't noticed at the harness shop the other day. She was a tall woman and he wasn't a tall man. Not that that mattered to her. In fact, she liked being able to walk beside him and look him eye-to-eye. Or she would if he wasn't making her so nervous, meeting her gaze, holding it every time she looked his way.

"Would you like something to drink? There's some of my *grossmammi*'s lemonade left. I'm partial to it. She adds a little fresh squeezed orange juice to it. And plenty of sugar, unlike someone else I know," he joked.

She kept walking, trying not to laugh, because it would only encourage him. In the last couple hours, she'd gone back and forth half a dozen times trying to decide if she was brave enough to ride home with Marshall or not. A part of her wanted to because, against her will, she found she liked him. Not only was he fun to be around, always laughing and joking, but he was also such a kind man. Not self-centered like so many single men. He gave out compliments freely and seemed endlessly supportive, even to those members of his team who obviously couldn't play softball.

And he was the most handsome man on the field. Or at least she thought he was. He wore the same clothing all of the other eligible young men wore: homemade dungaree pants, a short-sleeved shirt and a straw hat. But there was something about him that made her a little light-headed when she was able to steal a glance at him when he wasn't looking. Maybe it was how tightly his sleeves fitted around his biceps, or the way his hair met his neckline, plain to see when he'd thrown aside his hat early in the game to make a play at home plate.

The other reason she was seriously considering riding home with Marshall was because of Ginger's dare. Not having to do dishes for a week was very tempting. But it was more than that. Ginger didn't think she'd ride home with Marshall alone in his buggy. She didn't think Lovage was brave enough. Or fun enough. Ginger said Lovage wasn't the kind of girl Marshall would ever be interested in.

What if she proved her wrong?

"Would you like to stay a little while?" Marshall asked. "Before we head home? Sometimes there are games for the singles after families head out. Singing and such."

She glanced at him. "At home that was more for the younger couples." The minute the word *couples* came out of her mouth, she blushed profusely and looked away. She couldn't believe she'd just said that, suggesting they were in any way a couple. "I... I didn't mean—"

"That I don't like to have fun because I've reached the ancient age of thirty?" he asked. His tone was teasing.

"That we're a couple," she blurted, knowing her face must be bright red.

He slid his hands into the front pockets of his pants thoughtfully. "I don't mind if you tell people we're courting, Lovey."

Her eyes widened. "We are *not* courting, Marshall Byler. I... I don't even know if I'm riding home with you."

"Sure you are. I already spoke with your mother and Benjamin about what time they'd like to see you home. She makes a mean strawberry-rhubarb tart, your *mam*." He smacked his lips together. "I think it would put my grandmother's to the test."

"You asked my mother for permission to drive me home?" Lovage asked indignantly.

"Not really. I think you and I are both old enough that we don't need permission from our elders. We know our own minds. I was just chatting with them, letting them know they'll be seeing more of me, now that you and I are courting."

"We are not courting!" she told him. "I don't even know you."

He stopped and tilted his head, looking at her. "Are we going to do this again, Lovey?" He gave an exaggerated sigh. "This is how we're going to get to know each other. Learn each other's likes and dislikes and such." He frowned. "I don't even know what your favorite color is."

"Blue," she said, before she caught herself.

He grinned. "Blue, of course. I would have guessed that. Blue because of my eyes."

"Blue is not my favorite color because—" She groaned in frustration. She would have liked to have said he was conceited, but he came off not as conceited but as the most confident young man she'd ever met. Which made him the total opposite of her. Lovage was definitely not confident, particularly around men.

He started walking and she walked with him, mostly because she didn't know what else to do. Her gaze strayed to her family gathered at the picnic tables under the hickory trees. Her mother and Benjamin had passed the baskets to her brothers. They'd be in their two buggies soon, headed home. If Lovage was going with them, she needed to say so.

"So that's a no on staying for the games?" Marshall went on. "In that case, we can take the long way home. I have a courting buggy, you know. A cozy two-seater." He winked at her. "I like your way of thinking, Lovey."

"Marshall," Lovage said, so rattled she couldn't even speak.

Just then, two young women in pretty rose-colored dressed walked past them. They were Ginger's age and pretty, with freckled noses and blond hair. Sisters, Lovage guessed.

"Nice game, Marshall," the taller of the two cooed.

The other giggled. "We got here late, otherwise we could have played on your team, Marshall," she said.

Marshall grinned. "Thanks. You should definitely join us next time."

Lovage cut her eyes at him. These girls

were openly flirting with him! And he was flirting back. And—and it made her angry because *she* was walking with him. He had asked *her* to ride home with him. And she could be fun. She could flirt.

Maybe.

Gripping the catcher's mask in one hand, Lovage turned to Marshall. "Yes," she blurted, so nervous that it came out too loud. Too forward.

"Ya?" He looked at her, his blue eyes twinkling in a way that made Lovage feel a little woozy.

"Yes, I'll ride home with you. I just…" She walked away from him. "I have to talk to my parents."

"Sounds like a plan." He was smiling now. Smiling at her. "I need to make sure my little brother and grandmother are set to go, anyway."

Lovage had learned from Ginger that Marshall's grandmother lived with him and that he had been caring for her and his little brother since their father passed away a few years ago. Lovage had to admit, at least to herself, that the idea that he was being a father to his twelve-year-old brother was evidence of what a truly good man he was.

"Meet you at the picnic tables in a few minutes?" Marshall asked. "We'll say goodbye to everyone, thank the bishop and his wife for having us and then go."

Lovage nodded as she hurried away.

"See you in a few minutes, Lovey!" he called after her.

Chapter Four

"Beautiful night." Marshall strode beside Lovage toward the buggies lined up on the far side of Bishop Simon's barn. He'd already hitched up Toby when he had walked his grandmother to her buggy and checked to be sure Sam had hitched old Jake properly. Sam had seemed proud that Marshall had given him the responsibility of seeing Grossmammi home safely, though he was disappointed he wouldn't be the one driving. Their grandmother would take the reins. Sam was turning out to be an excellent driver, but it would be nearly dark by the time they arrived home, and dusk was the most dangerous time of day to be driving a horse and buggy on the roads. Englisher drivers were too unpredictable. Marshall knew it was his duty to teach Sam how to navigate the busy roadway, but his first responsibility was to his family's safety.

Marshall smiled to himself as he glanced at Lovey, walking beside him. He felt like he didn't have a care in the world tonight. His team had won the softball game, he'd had an excellent chat with Lovey's parents, and now he was taking his sweetheart home alone in his buggy. The fact that she hadn't agreed to be his sweetheart yet was a minor detail. Marshall knew, in his heart of hearts, Lovey was the woman for him. He'd recognized it the moment he saw her at the harness shop. Spending time near her this afternoon had only given him more confidence in his choice.

Watching Lovey interact with her siblings and stepbrothers while she'd shared the cookout feast with her family had given him the opportunity to see what a fine sister and daughter she was. She was attentive not just to her siblings, but to her mother, as well. More than once, Marshall, who'd been watching her from his family's picnic blanket across the yard, saw Lovey jump up to do a task, allowing her mother to relax and enjoy getting to know her new neighbors. Then, watching Lovey play softball had shown him yet another side of her. She was competitive, but not in a sour way, and she tried her best, even when she knew chances were she wouldn't be successful. And while definitely on the shy side, she was willing to offer her opinion when asked. She was a smart player, kind and fair to the others on her own team as well as his. The fact that she was a good softball player was just a bonus.

He glanced at Lovey, who was walking with her head down. "Beautiful night for a *long* ride," he told her, slipping his thumbs behind his suspenders, stretching them and releasing them.

"It's not all that far to our farm," she responded. "Less than two miles, I'd say."

"Benjamin told me he turned in around ten. Said he and Rosemary liked all of his chicks in the house by then." Marshall pulled out a pocket watch that had been his father's and *his* father's before that, and checked the time. "We've got more than an hour before your parents will be expecting you. Which means we can take the long way home."

"Why would we go the long way?" she asked, sounding perplexed.

Just the sound of her voice made Marshall want to take her hand in his. She looked so pretty this evening in a blue, calf-length dress, the color of the cornflowers that grew in his grandmother's flower beds. Wisps of soft brown hair peeked from beneath her white prayer kapp pinned securely to her head. And she had a little smudge of dirt on her chin, which, in his eyes, made her even prettier. He could tell that Lovey wasn't one of those single women who spent their days sitting on their father's porches waiting for men to court them. Lovey wasn't afraid to get dirty on the softball field, which meant she wouldn't mind getting dirty in their garden, weeding beside him. In his mind's eye, he could just imagine the two of them in the early morning, tidying the beds, talking and laughing, enjoying the sunshine and each other's company.

That was the kind of wife Marshall wanted. A woman who could be his partner. When he lay in bed alone at night, he imagined having the kind of marriage his parents had shared. The kind where husband and wife tried to lighten each other's load. He didn't necessarily believe that opposites attracted; it was important for a man and his wife to have the same religious convictions, the same morals. But he *did* think that a man's weaknesses should be shored up by his wife's strengths, and vice versa. While he was outgoing, Lovey was more reserved. She was cautious, while he had been known to make snap decisions.

In his eyes, the combination of those traits would only make them a better team to experience the joys and the trials they would face in their life together. He truly believed that was God's intention when he had created man and wife.

"Why would I want to take the long way?" Marshall asked her. "So I can spend as much time as possible with you," he explained.

She finally glanced at him. The look on her face was quizzical. "But why would you want to do that?"

He smiled, not entirely sure if she was serious or not. Did she really not know how beautiful she was? How smart and capable? "Because I want to get to know you. Because I enjoy being with you," he told her. "Is that so hard to believe?"

She narrowed her green eyes. "*Ya*, a little."

He tilted his head back and laughed hard, and when he looked at her again, she was smiling at him. It was a smile that warmed his heart. One look at the smile that was for him alone, and he made his mind up that once they were in his cozy, two-seater buggy and away from prying eyes, he was definitely going to hold her hand. Or at least give it his best shot.

"Tomorrow is visiting Sunday for our

church," he told her as they rounded the corner of the barn to where the buggies were parked. "I was wondering what you would think about me bringing my grandmother and brother by your place. Benjamin made the invitation. To stop by and say hello if we were in the neighborhood." He chuckled. "Of course, obviously we're in the neighborhood. It's an easy walk between my place and yours. In fact, if it's nice—"

Marshall halted midsentence, staring in disbelief at what he was seeing.

Just beyond his cousin John Mary Byler's buggy was his own. It was a handsome two-seater that he had purchased when he was in his early twenties. It was a perfect buggy for courting, because it was light and fast and open, so no young woman's parents need be concerned for their daughter's reputation. It was perfect to take Lovey on what might be considered their first date. Perfect, except that sitting in the middle of the bench seat was a boy of about ten. A boy he was pretty sure he recognized from Benjamin's harness shop. And from Lovey's family's picnic blanket earlier in the evening.

He turned to look at Lovey, confident she knew better than he did what was going. She was grinning, and he found her smile infectious, even though he was pretty sure she'd gotten the best of him here.

"And who might this young man be?" he asked Lovage.

The boy had a shaggy head of brown hair, a cute grin and green eyes that were familiar to Marshall. "I'm Jesse. Lovey's brother." He pointed at her.

"I hope you don't mind, Marshall." Lovey's mouth twitched into a playful smile as she rounded the buggy, giving his horse a rub on the nose as she went by. "You asked me if I wanted to ride home with you. You didn't say I couldn't bring my little brother."

He glanced away and then back at her, not angry, but amused that his Lovey would play such a trick on him. "Are you asking me if he can ride squeezed in between us?" Marshall asked, meeting her gaze.

Her green eyes twinkled with amusement. "That's not a problem, is it, Marshall?"

"Not at all, Lovey." He chuckled and walked over to unhitch Toby from the hitching post. "Not a bit."

Against Lovage's will, she found herself relaxing on the buggy ride home. With Jesse seated between them, actually squeezed in between them, as Marshall had observed, she felt more comfortable with Marshall, and with herself. With Jesse there to act as a buffer, she didn't feel so self-conscious. Usually, when she was alone with a man, she was uncomfortable, worrying so much about what she said or did that she never had a good time. Not that she'd had that many dates in her life.

Tonight was different and she didn't know why. Was it Marshall that made it different? Instead of worrying about where she put her hands or how often she looked at him, she found herself laughing at his jokes and enjoying his stories, which seemed endless. She'd laughed so hard when he told her about his grandmother catching one of their old hens and insisting she was going to put it in the stew pot. And she couldn't help smiling when he related a story about the neighbor's baby goat he had saved from a dog, nursed back to health and given to his little brother as a companion.

"I'm not exaggerating when I tell you the kid follows him around like a dog," Marshall told her. He glanced down at Jesse, seated between them. "You're welcome to come over and meet Petunia yourself, if you like."

Jesse giggled. "Who names a goat *Petunia*?"

Marshall, the leather reins gripped in his

broad hands, leaned over as if letting him in on a secret. "Our grandmother named her because the first go-round with a name..." He raised his eyebrows. "Sam was calling him Peter. You see the fault in that, don't you?"

Jesse broke into another peal of giggles. "It was a girl goat, not a boy goat."

"I like your brother," Marshall told Lovage, talking over Jesse's head. "He's smart, this one. Catches on fast."

Jesse giggled again and Lovage couldn't help smiling. When she'd decided to have Jesse ride home with them to serve as a chaperone, as she'd explained to her mother, she'd half expected Marshall to change his mind. A single man as good-looking, as charming, as Marshall could have had his pick of any single girl there that night. Her sister Ginger indeed would have ridden with him. Lovage bet those two girls who were flirting with him would have let him drive them home, too. And none of them would have brought their little brother along.

But Marshall hadn't changed his mind. In fact, he'd had a good sense of humor about the whole thing. Not only had he agreed Jesse could ride with them, but he'd been kind to him, talking as much to him as to her. Marshall had taken the long way to Benjamin's farm, but it seemed to Lovey as if the hour had gone by in minutes. One minute she and Marshall were pulling onto the road from Bishop Simon's and the next, they were turning at the Miller's Harness Shop sign that her sister Nettie had painted. It was a beautiful handmade wood sign with a buggy in the background, indicating Benjamin and his son Levi also dabbled in buggy-making.

Lovage almost felt disappointed when their big white, rambling two-story farmhouse came into view. She couldn't recall the last time she'd so enjoyed a buggy ride. Or the company of a man.

Marshall eased his horse in the side yard near the house and jumped down.

As he walked up to tie Toby to the hitching post, Lovage turned to her brother and said quietly, "Mind your manners. Be sure to thank Marshall for giving you a ride home from the game."

"Ya," Jesse responded, beaming.

Lovage stood to get out of the buggy before Marshall reached her side, but she wasn't quick enough. And there he was, looking up at her, his hand out to help her down.

Lovage seriously considered not taking his hand, and climbing down herself. But before she could make up her mind, he caught her fingers with his and she felt a warmth that brought a rush of heat to her cheeks.

"Thank you for the ride home," Jesse said from behind Marshall. "You think it would be okay if I came tomorrow morning, after chores, to see Petunia?"

"Jesse, you shouldn't invite yourself," Lovage admonished. Her sneakers touched the ground and she found herself almost disappointed when Marshall took his hand away from hers.

"You're *velcom* for the ride. Anytime. Of course you can come tomorrow morning. As long as you have your mother's permission," Marshall told Jesse. He looked back at Lovage, shrugging his shoulders, which seemed even broader to her today than they had the first day they'd met. "He wasn't inviting himself. I already invited you, right, Jesse?"

Jesse beamed again.

Lovage bunched the fabric of her skirt in her hands. "Thank you for the ride home," she said, trying to think of a way to sidestep Marshall and make her escape to the house.

"You're welcome," he answered. But he didn't move, effectively keeping her pinned, her back to the buggy. "But I'm not done with you." He glanced over his shoulder at her little brother. "Off with you, now, Jesse. I want to talk to your sister alone."

Jesse yanked off his straw hat and took off toward the side porch. "Thanks again, Marshall. See you tomorrow."

When he was gone, Marshall turned back to Lovage. "That was pretty clever of you, agreeing to ride home with me and *then* inviting your little brother." He was smiling slyly.

A mosquito buzzed around her head, but she didn't want to swat at it and look foolish to him. "*Ya*, it was, wasn't it?" She crossed her arms over her chest, feeling awkward. He was standing so close to her that even though it was dark, she could see his blue eyes watching her.

He smirked, narrowing his eyes. "You don't really think you're the first girl I've ever dated who brought along a chaperone, do you? I walked out with a girl from Rose Valley who took her elderly aunt with her everywhere we went."

Lovage covered her mouth with her hand to keep from giggling. "We're not dating," she told him.

He rolled his eyes. "Of course we are. You rode home with me in my buggy. Half the county saw you. By the end of tomorrow, the rest of the county will know by way of the

Amish telegraph." He stepped back. "Come on. Let me walk you to the door. I think someone is watching us from the front window." He nodded in the direction of the house.

Lovage looked over his shoulder just in time to see the curtain fall over one of the parlor windows.

"Which leads me to a question I've wanted to ask you since you threw Will out at third base."

"Marshall, we're not dating." She shook her head. "You asked the new girl in town to ride home with you. I did. Your curiosity is satisfied, and now we can both let this go."

"Oh, no. My curiosity is in no way satisfied." They followed a brick walk around the corner of the house, toward the side porch that opened into the big country kitchen that Benjamin had remodeled with all new cabinets when they moved in. "In fact," Marshall told her, "I'm all the more intrigued by you. Would you like to go for ice cream Thursday? Maybe we'll have supper first, then ice cream. Or the other way around, if you like. You can bring Jesse. I'll bring my grandmother. That way we'll have two chaperones." He cut his eyes at her. "I have to tell you, Lovey. That was smart of you to bring Jesse with us on our first date. Because had he not been sitting between us, I would have tried to hold your hand."

She looked at him, not sure if she was flattered or shocked that he would say such a thing. Where she came from, couples were encouraged not to hold hands or to hug. Kissing was most definitely frowned upon. Courting was intended to be a way for couples to get to know each other, to find out how compatible they were. But unlike in the English world, in the Amish community, physical contact between a man and a woman was meant for a husband and wife only.

He stepped in so close to her that she could feel his warm breath on her face. "Oh, Lovey, don't tell me you were thinking the same thing? Is that why you brought Jesse along, so you wouldn't be tempted to hold my hand on our first date?"

She gave a little laugh. She'd never met anyone who said such ridiculous things. At least not to her. "I certainly was not going to hold your hand," she told him indignantly.

"Good, because I think we should wait a few dates. No need to rush things. Well…not in that way." He started walking again, then stopped. "Which, in a roundabout way, brings me to what I wanted to ask you."

The propane light beside the door on

the side porch flared and Lovage caught a glimpse of Ginger slipping back into the house.

"I should go in," Lovage said, suddenly feeling nervous. "We have family prayer at ten before Benjamin and Mam say good-night." She pressed her lips together. She didn't really want to say good-night, but that was girlish folly. She'd had a good time, but it was best she and Marshall parted now. For whatever reason he'd asked to take her home, surely he was content now. She'd be kidding herself to think he really wanted to take her for ice cream, even if it was with his grand-mother.

"Marshall, my family—"

"Lovey." He caught her hand. His grip was firm and warm. "Will you marry me?"

"What?" She shook her head. "*Ne*— what—" She was so flabbergasted she didn't even know what to say.

It wasn't until he squeezed her hand that she realized he was still holding it. She pulled her hand from his. "No, I won't m—" She stopped and started again. "Marshall Byler, what would possess you to ask me to marry you?" she demanded, feeling embarrassed, angry and a little giddy at the same time.

What kind of game was he playing that he would say such a thing?

"What would possess me?" He looked at her earnestly. "I asked because I want to marry. I'm in love with you, Lovey."

"How can you be in love with me?" She opened her arms wide. "You don't even know me."

"Which is why you should go get ice cream with me Thursday." He said it with such sincerity that she half believed he meant what he was saying.

Motion in a different parlor window than before caught her eyes. She grabbed the hem of his sleeve and tugged, moving them out of the line of vision of whoever was spying on her. "I have to go inside," she whispered loudly.

"So Thursday is good for you?" he asked.

"Ya..." She pressed her hand to her forehead. He had her so flustered. "*Ne*, Marshall. You don't want to— I don't want to—"

"You don't like ice cream?" He took a step back, clutching both hands to his heart, looking as if he was heartbroken.

She closed her eyes, shaking her head, then opened them again. "Of course I like ice cream."

"Good." They reached the steps that led up

to the kitchen porch. "When I see you tomorrow afternoon, we can make plans. I know you said hello to my grandmother when everyone was making introductions before we ate tonight, but it's important to me that you two get to know each other before you and I are married."

Lovage felt as if she was on a merry-go-round at the state fair. She threw her hands up in the air. "Now we're talking about marriage again?" she asked incredulously.

"Ne." He held his hand up, palm out. "We're not. It's okay. No need to answer me tonight. You're right. No need to be in any hurry." He took a step back. "Thank you for such a wonderful evening, Lovey. I'll see you tomorrow when we make the rounds in the neighborhood. My grandmother loves visiting Sundays."

Lovage watched him walk away, trying to think of something to holler to him. But she didn't know *what* to say. Except maybe to ask him if he'd lost his mind, asking a woman he didn't know to marry him.

Just as he reached his buggy, he turned back. "Tell your *mam* three o'clock is fine for us. And we'll bring the lemonade," he added.

"Not funny," she called after him, trying not to laugh.

Lovage stood on the steps watching Marshall until he turned his buggy around in the barnyard and headed back down the driveway. He waved as he went by and she felt a strange sense of light-headedness.

When she couldn't hear hoofbeats any longer, she reached for the kitchen door, only to have it pulled out of her hand.

"I can't believe you actually did it!" Ginger said, filling the doorway.

Lovage walked past her. "Close the door or you'll let the bugs in. One week of dishes. You owe one week."

"How was it? How was *he*?" Ginger followed her into the big country kitchen, which was dominated by two tables that could seat all thirteen members of their new family, as well as three or four guests, without even putting the leaves in them. The room smelled fresh and clean, no doubt thanks to her mother's little bundle of freshly cut mint on the windowsill. "I couldn't believe it when *mam* told me you took Jesse with you."

"He was my chaperone. A girl is better off to take a chaperone with her. Then no tongues can wag." Lovage reached the sink and turned to her sister, holding up her finger. "You're not getting out of doing my dishes. You didn't say I had to ride home alone with him." She reached for a pint-size Ball jar and filled it with water.

Ginger stood with one hand on her hip, staring at Lovage, making her feel uncomfortable.

Her younger sister crossed her arms. "Don't feel bad if he doesn't offer to take you home again. I heard from *mam*, who heard from old Grace Swartzentruber, that Lynita was just saying last week that Marshall wants to start dating again. Since his father's passing. It will probably be a different girl every week."

Lovage tipped the jar, taking a long drink of the cool, sweet well water. Benjamin had told her that he'd had a new well put in when he purchased the property. It was a deep well, which he was told would bring up the best water in the county, and she had to agree he may have been right. The water certainly was good, not like the water they'd had back in New York that sometimes tasted brackish.

"There's a singing Thursday night." Ginger swayed her hips, deep in thought. "I wonder if he'll ask me to go."

"Doubt it," Lovage said.

Ginger frowned. "What? You don't think he'll ask me because you didn't suit him? You think he thinks all the Stutzman girls are alike, do you?"

"I don't think he'll ask you to the singing because he's busy Thursday." Lovage took another sip of water, not knowing what had gotten into her.

Ginger pouted. "I don't understand."

"He won't be asking you to the singing because he asked to take me to get ice cream."

Ginger stood there in the kitchen, her mouth agape, as Lovage rinsed the glass, put it in the drain and then headed into the parlor to join the family for evening prayers.

Chapter Five

"I can't believe I'm making baby clouts and gowns again," Rosemary remarked, the straight pins in her mouth muddling her words.

Head down, Lovage pumped the treadle on her mother's sewing machine with both feet, easing the seam of a baby gown through the foot. It had turned out to be a rainy day, and while her sisters were busy giving the kitchen and mudroom a good scrub top to bottom, their mother had asked Lovage to join her in her sewing room to help with some baby clothing she had cut out but hadn't had time to stitch.

Most of the rooms in the new house looked very different than the ones in their old farmhouse in New York. And Lovage understood why her mother would do that, because this was Benjamin's and her house; a new house, a new husband, a new life. There was even a new baby on the way. But her *mam*'s sewing room was almost identical to the one she'd left behind. Lovage wondered if it was an acknowledgment to her father? Maybe to the life Mam once had?

A battered antique pine table under the window held a pile of fabric meant for baby clothing, as well as cut and pinned lengths of cloth that, once stitched together, looked like it would be a pink everyday dress for some-one. Lovage guessed it might be for her sis-ter Tarragon. About to turn eighteen, Tara had had a sudden growth spurt in the spring and had been making do with her sisters' dresses, according to a letter she had sent to Lovage while she was still in New York. Lovage knew her sister, the youngest of the five girls, would be pleased to have a brand-new dress of her own, especially since she often wore hand-me-downs.

Lovage lifted the foot on the old Singer sewing machine to cut the thread, and gazed around the room, feeling nostalgic for the old farmhouse where she and her siblings had been born. Nearly square, with two large win-dows, this sewing room, like the old one, was painted a pale blue, with a blue-white-and-yellow rag rug in the middle of the floor. There were two rocking chairs placed side by side where sisters, or mother and daughter, could sit and knit. One wall boasted an oversize walnut cabinet rescued from a twentieth-century millinery shop, and open drawers revealed an assortment of various sizes of thread, needles, scissors and paper patterns. A small knotty-pine table with turned legs stood between the windows, a big terra-cotta planter filled with fresh herbs and flowers in its center.

"The Lord works in mysterious ways," her mother went on. "That's what Benjamin says. That we should accept His gifts without question, but I have to admit there are times…"

Rosemary went on with her musings, but Lovage was lost in her own thoughts. And all she could think about was Marshall. True to his word, he had brought his grandmother and brother on Sunday to visit with her family. Just as in her community in New York, the Old Order Amish churches in Kent County held church in someone's home every other Sunday. On the other Sundays, visiting Sundays, they spent time with family and friends. Like church Sundays, visiting Sunday was a day of rest and prayer. No work was done, except what was required to care for the animals in the barns. There was no gardening, no cleaning of stalls, no repairs made. Most families didn't even cook, but instead, particularly in the summer months, relied for sustenance on salads and sliced meats prepared on Saturday.

It had been a picture-perfect day for visiting, and Lovage's family had spent hours at picnic tables under the giant hickory trees in their side yard. There, they'd chatted with neighbors and spent time reconnecting with each other after a busy week. When Marshall and his family arrived, Rosemary was just serving an afternoon snack. Marshall had brought not only lemonade, but also fresh chicken salad, made with pimento and cheddar cheese of all things, and tiny croissant rolls that Lynita had baked herself. The snack turned into an early supper, and they had eaten the chicken sandwiches with an assortment of cold salads, including German potato, Waldorf and macaroni. There were also bowls of pickled cucumbers, a five-bean succotash-and-pepper slaw. And then, when the two families thought they could eat no more. Benjamin produced trays of huge slices of watermelon he'd chilled in the well house.

After the meal, Marshall had asked Lovage if she wanted to go for a walk with him in

the garden. He had teased that he wanted to
see if the herbs she had planted the previous week had survived. She had hesitated,
but then Ginger had piped up, "I'll go," and
popped off the bench she'd been sitting on
under the trees.

So Lovage, Marshall and Ginger had taken
a walk through the fenced-in garden and then
around the farm, and Marshall and Ginger
had chatted. Mostly, Ginger had talked. At
first, Lovage was annoyed that her sister
was monopolizing the conversation, but then
she'd realized it was probably just as well,
because her sister was so good at conversation and she wasn't. Marshall would certainly
enjoy Ginger's banter more than any awkward exchange she and he would have. So
Lovage had stayed mostly quiet, only speaking when Marshall had asked her something
directly. And then, when they'd joined the
others under the hickory trees again, Lynita
had been ready to leave, as they were expected at her great-niece's house. Marshall
had said goodbye without mentioning going
for ice cream with him Thursday, and Lovage
decided she was okay with that. Whatever
reason he had asked her out in the first place
had run its course. For all she knew, when
Ginger was talking to him alone just before

he left, they could have decided to go to the singing at the schoolhouse on Thursday instead. And she couldn't blame Marshall. He and Ginger had gotten along well. They had seemed so at ease together that she wouldn't be surprised if they were soon walking out.

"Lovey, are you listening to me? You're a million miles away."

Lovage blinked, glanced down at the unfinished seam of the baby gown, and then back at her mother. "I'm sorry, Mam. Gathering wool again, I suppose." She chuckled and began to pump the treadle that would turn the needle.

"I was saying that Benjamin and I were impressed Sunday with your young man. He's a little older than you are, but your father was ten years older than I was and it was never a problem. Lynita said he's thirty. Thirty-one on Christmas Eve. Not too old for you at all."

"He's not *my* young man," Lovage said over the rhythmic sound of the sewing machine.

Her mother set down the baby cap she'd pinned together and planted her hands on her broad hips. "Hannah Lovage Stutzman. A week ago, you were telling me you didn't want to talk about marriage because no man would ever be interested in you." She gestured with one hand. "Now a possible suitor—a handsome one, I have to say—pays you some mind and you're going to turn your nose up at him?"

"I think he likes Ginger." Lovage tried not to pout.

"Everyone likes Ginger. That doesn't mean everyone wants to marry her. And Marshall Byler didn't come to see Ginger on Sunday. He came to see you. And he took *you* home from the softball game. I think he's smitten with you."

Lovage felt her cheeks grow warm. "He is most definitely not—" She stopped peddling, realizing she was sewing the seam crooked. "He's not smitten with me." She kept her head down as she pulled the baby gown out from the foot of the sewing machine and reached for her seam ripper. "Why would he be?"

"Atch, kuche." Rosemary sighed. "I was afraid of this."

"Afraid of what?" Still Lovage didn't look at her mother. She didn't look at her for fear she'd tear up. Because as much as she wanted to say she wasn't interested in Marshall Byler, it would be a lie—to her *mam* and herself. Because the truth was, the more time she spent with Marshall, the more she liked him. He was smart and funny and kind, and he seemed to enjoy each moment of the day to its fullest. The hours she'd spent with him were the best she could remember in a very long time. Maybe even ever.

"You know, *dochtah*, you did the right thing, not agreeing to marry Ishmael Slabaugh."

Lovage set her jaw and tugged at the errant stitches with the sharp seam ripper with a force that wasn't necessary. "I know that, Mam."

"He wasn't the right man for you." She made a sound between her teeth. "To tell you he was asking for your hand because Betsy Miller turned him down? Shame on him. Shame—"

"Mam, please," Lovage interrupted. "I don't want to talk about this. The past is the past. Forget what is behind and strain toward what is ahead. Isn't that what Preacher Clyde said in his sermon last time you visited me in New York? I think it's from Philippians."

"It was wrong of Ishmael to ask that way, to tell you about Betsy Miller turning him down, but, daughter, it was wrong of you to think it meant you weren't good enough for him. That you aren't good enough for—"

"Ouch!" Lovage cried, dropping the seam ripper. She watched blood bubble up from her index finger and then put her injured finger into her mouth with a groan. She'd slipped and poked herself, and now there was a tiny spot of blood on the new baby gown. "I'm sorry," she said, surprisingly close to tears. "I've gotten blood on the fabric."

Rosemary slipped the tiny piece of clothing out from under her fingers and studied it. "*Ach*, nothing that a drop of peroxide won't fix. Now listen to me, daughter." She took Lovage's chin with her free hand and tilted it upward, forcing Lovey to look at her.

"Ishmael wasn't the husband for you. He never was. And him asking you that way, you telling him no, doesn't make you less worthy a bride to another man. In fact, it makes you worthier." She met her daughter's gaze with steady green eyes.

Lovage lowered her own. She wanted to believe what her mother said was true, and logically, she knew it was so. But that didn't keep her from sometimes wondering if it wouldn't have been smarter to accept Ishmael's proposal. "Mam, please."

Rosemary released Lovage's chin and picked up the dropped seam ripper. "It makes you worthier because you have respect for yourself. Because you refuse to be second best to a man."

Lovey looked down at her lap, nursing

her stinging finger. "Can we please not talk about Ishmael?"

"What did I do?" Rosemary exclaimed, setting down the things in her hands. "Where did I go wrong, Lovey, that you never think you're good enough? That you think you don't deserve a kind, loving husband, the same as the rest of us?"

Lovage shook her head, feeling guilty that her mother felt that her struggles with self-esteem had anything to do with the way she had raised her. "You did nothing wrong," she said softly, trying to get control of her emotions. She was on the verge of tears and she didn't even know why.

That wasn't true. She *did* know why she was distressed and this wasn't about Ishmael; it was about Marshall. Maybe she was upset because she'd never expected to feel this way about a man and it scared her. It scared her because she was having a hard time believing Marshall liked her, wanted to be with her, even though he'd come right out and said it. Even though he'd proposed marriage their very first date. At the thought of it, she almost giggled out loud. And then suddenly she felt her heart buoyed. Two men had asked her to marry them in the last year. How many women her age could say that?

"Lovage, look at me," her mother pressed.

Lovage slowly lifted her gaze until she met her mother's.

Rosemary reached out and gently tugged on one of Lovage's prayer *kapp* strings, which fell just below her chin. "You are worthy of a good husband, of love. And I truly believe that God has a man in mind for you. So don't be foolish. Don't push Marshall away. Because what if he's the one God means for you to marry? I think God leads us to the answers to our prayers, but He doesn't force us to accept His gifts. We all have the free will to accept love or not."

Rosemary seemed lost in her thoughts for a moment and then she went on. "I've not said this to anyone else, but you know, when Benjamin asked me to be his wife, I argued with him. I argued with myself. I argued with God. Benjamin was my beloved Ethan's best friend. It seemed wrong to marry him. To love him," she said softly. "But that was God's intention. It took a lot of praying and Benjamin's kindness and patience for me to come to accept that."

Lovage stared at the foot of the sewing machine. "But what if God means for me to be single? To stay here and care for you. With the new baby coming—"

"God means for my husband to care for me," Rosemary interrupted, now sounding exasperated. "You need to accept Benjamin as my husband."

Lovage looked up, surprised by her mother's words. "Of course I accept him as your husband. I love Benjamin. What would make you think I don't? Because never once did I disagree with your choice, Mam," she said passionately. "I do believe God intended you to be together."

Rosemary crossed her arms over her round belly. "I'd like to think that's true."

"It is true." Lovage rose. "I love Benjamin," she said firmly. "And I love him more because he loves you."

"Then you have to accept that this child and I—" she rubbed her swollen abdomen "—are Benjamin's responsibilities. As my husband and the babe's father." Rosemary sighed. "*Ach*, daughter." She put her arms out to Lovage. "I know as my firstborn you feel a responsibility to me, but your responsibility is to yourself. You—"

A knock on the door frame of the sewing room made them both look up. It was Jesse. "Got a customer at the shop, Lovey," he said. "Wants to see you."

Lovage frowned. "Isn't Ginger in the shop?

And Jacob and Joshua? I'm not supposed to be working today."

"Said he won't see anyone but you." Jesse pressed his lips together. "Sent me to fetch you."

"I'm sewing for Mam. Is there a problem with something he had repaired?"

Jesse had a strange look on his face. "Said he'd only see you," he repeated.

Lovage glanced at her mother.

"Go," Rosemary said with a wave. "And put a Band-Aid on that finger before you come back." She picked up a section of the pink dress on the table and slipped onto the stool at the sewing machine. "I promised to get that dress stitched for Tara before the singing tomorrow night, but she'll have a fit if you bleed on it."

Annoyed to be pulled away from the conversation with her mother, but also curious as to what customer wanted to see her, Lovage grabbed a black umbrella at the back door and followed Jesse to the harness shop. The moment she walked into the store, she turned around and looked down at Jesse. It was Marshall Byler. And he was talking to Ginger. Who was giggling and leaning across the counter toward him.

"Marshall wanted me?" she whispered

harshly to her brother. Without realizing she was doing it, she reached up to make sure her *kapp* was on properly, then down to smooth her dress. "Why didn't you say it was him?"

Jesse sheepishly held up a dollar bill.

Glancing over her shoulder at her little brother, Lovage strode toward the customer counter where Marshall waited. "You should probably go before you're in trouble," she told Jesse.

He took off.

When she reached the counter, Lovage looked at her little sister. "I didn't know you were working out front. You could have saved me the trouble of walking all the way from the house."

Ginger took a step back. "I should get back to work," she told Marshall.

He nodded, offering a quick smile. "Good to see you."

Lovage waited until her sister went through the door into the workroom before she turned back to Marshall. "Ginger couldn't have helped you?"

"Didn't want Ginger," he said, his tone playful. "I wanted you."

A warmth washed over as she thought about what her mother had said to her. *He came to see you, not Ginger.* "You sent my little brother to get me without telling me it was you?"

"Not his fault," Marshall said to her. "If you want to be angry with someone, be angry with me."

She exhaled, trying not to smile. "I'm not angry with him. When I was his age, I'd have done the same for a dollar."

He grinned.

"Still, you could have just sent him for me, saying you wanted me." She crossed her arms over her chest, glad she'd changed her dress midmorning after spilling maple syrup on herself. "It wouldn't have cost you your hard-earned money."

"I was afraid you might not come." He rapped his knuckles on the counter and then pressed both palms to the smooth surface and leaned forward. "Would you have come out if you'd known it was me, Lovey?"

He'd shaved and had on a lavender short-sleeved shirt that looked as if his grandmother had pressed it for him. And he was wearing his good straw hat, not the one with the piece out of the brim that he'd worn the first time they met.

She glanced at the finger she'd injured, wanting to make sure she wasn't bleeding on her dress. "Maybe," she confessed. "Maybe not." She looked up at him. "What do you need? I'm busy. My mother needs my help."

"I like that blue dress on you," he said, holding her gaze. "You look pretty in blue, even though your eyes are green. A nice green. Not muddy like some."

Against her will, Lovage felt her cheeks flush. Marshall was flirting with her. Again. Maybe he really did like her. "I have things to do." She fought a smile. "You asked to speak to me, and here I am."

He sighed and stood to his full height again. "I came to see if my *britchen* strap was ready."

"It's not."

He laughed, gesturing with one hand in the direction of the workshop. "You didn't even check yet."

"I don't have to. I told you when it would be done.Five business days." She moved a stapler on the counter from one side of the cash register to the other. "Probably be next week."

He grinned again, his blue eyes twinkling with mischief. "I knew it wouldn't be ready."

She raised one eyebrow. "Then why did you come?"

He shrugged. "Not all that busy at home today, not with the rain. I'm working on building a tack room in our barn. I'll show it to you when you come for supper."

"I didn't know I was coming to supper."

"Sure you are. For Sam's birthday, next weekend. Your whole family is coming." He leaned on the counter again. "Anyway, the strap was just an excuse to see you. I know we're going for ice cream tomorrow, but I couldn't wait to see you."

His words surprised her. "Wait, we're still going for ice cream?"

"Of course," he said, seemingly genuinely taken aback. "Well, supper and ice cream. My grandmother likes fancy fast-food chicken." He frowned. "Why did you think we weren't going?"

Lovage pressed her lips together. She wanted to tell him that she didn't think they were going because she knew he couldn't really be interested in her. Not someone like her who took her responsibilities to her family seriously, someone who *wasn't fun*.

Marshall held her gaze again; he had the bluest eyes, like the color of the sky on a hot summer day. A long moment passed before he tapped the countertop with his knuckles. "Also, church is at Barnabas Gruber's on Sunday. I'd like to drive you home after."

"Drive me?" She gave a little laugh. "The

Grubers live on the road behind me. It's plenty close enough to walk."

He shrugged. "Good idea. I'll walk you home." He gave the stapler she'd moved a little push with his finger. "I'll pick you up about five on Thursday? I hired a van. Route 13 is too busy to take Toby out on. Any horse, really. Grossmammi and Sam are coming. You should bring Jesse."

"You really want me to have supper and ice cream with you?" she asked, still feeling like she should be suspicious. After all, who would choose her over Ginger? "There's a singing at the Fishers', you know. Because Asa King had to cancel hers last Friday night."

"*Ya*, I know there's a singing. Ginger just told me all about it." He flashed her another handsome smile. "But Grossmammi is looking forward to her chicken nuggets. So, five o'clock on Thursday?"

Lovage knew the smart thing was to end this flirtation, this...whatever it was, right now. She knew a man like Marshall couldn't really be interested romantically in her. Even if he did, how long would that last once he realized how dull she was? And then she would be crushed. But she liked him so much and he was so cute and he *seemed* sincere.

"Okay if Jesse brings his friend Adam, too?" she said in a rush of words. "Adam Raber from over at the next crossroad. I'll pay for us myself, of course," she added.

"It's definitely okay if Jesse brings a friend, and you will do no such thing. My treat." He hesitated and then said softly, "See you tomorrow, Lovey."

"It's Lovage," she called after him as he walked away.

"I know," he called back.

And then he laughed and she felt warm to the very tips of her toes inside her black canvas sneakers.

Chapter Six

After the final church service of the day, Marshall stood in the Grubers' barnyard with a group of single men, discussing the weather and the state of their wheat and soybean crops. As he listened to the conversation, he scanned the backyard for Lovey. They'd barely spoken a dozen words all day, but that was just because during services, the men sat separately from the women. Then when it had been time for dinner at the long tables set up under the trees, Lovey had been busy helping to serve the meal. Marshall had wanted to wait to eat until the second sitting, when most of the women, including Lovey, would eat, but he'd gotten roped into a conversation with their new preacher and had ended up sitting with a group of men at the first sitting. The whole meal, Marshall had kept his eye on Lovey, and though they'd made eye contact several times and she'd smiled at him, she'd not come to his table, not even to see if he needed more water or iced tea.

They'd had a good week, he and Lovey. After a successful trip out for dinner with his grandmother, Sam, Jesse and his friend, he'd managed to see her again on Friday. He'd gone late in the day, just before supper, under the guise of checking on his *britchen* strap. It wasn't ready yet, of course, but she'd ended up standing in the barnyard talking to him until her stepfather had closed up shop and the dinner bell rang. Lovey was still definitely a little shy with him, but he could see her warming up. And the more time he spent with her, the more time he wanted to spend with her.

"What do you say?" Joshua, one of Lovey's stepbrothers, asked, poking Marshall in the ribs. "You have time for a little project?"

Marshall glanced at Josh, feeling guilty that he hadn't been paying attention. Last he'd heard, they were still talking about the rising cost of seeds and whether or not GMO seeds were a necessary evil of the modern world they often struggled to remain apart from. "Sorry?" he said.

"The greenhouse. Will was telling you

about it at dinner. We've a mind to build Rosemary a greenhouse. Will's already drawn up the plans. We just need a couple of extra hands. We're thinking we can squeeze a few hours in here and there when we're not busy."

Marshall's gaze strayed to the house again as he plucked at his suspenders. Women were coming and going, with children trailing behind them. Everyone was putting away the last of the dishes and loading the benches on the church wagon, which moved from house to house, depending on who was hosting. "*Ya*, sure. I'm in. I can spare a few hours here and there." He glanced in the direction of the backyard again, hoping Lovey hadn't already left. He thought he'd been clear that he wanted to walk her home.

Will, Lovey's stepbrother who he was good friends with, laughed and took off his black, wide-brimmed Sunday hat to wipe his forehead with a handkerchief. "If you're looking for my sister, she was in the kitchen last I saw. Your grandmother was questioning her pretty hard."

"Which one?" Jeb Fisher, Josh and Jacob's friend, joked. "That Ginger has a mighty cute smile." He slipped his thumbs behind his suspenders. "I've a mind to ask her to let me take her home, next time my parents have a singing."

Jacob gave Josh a playful push. "Aw, you been saying that for weeks. Just can't get up the nerve, can you?"

The other fellows joined in on the laughter and Josh looked over at Marshall again. "We're talking about our oldest sister, Lovey. Been seeing a lot of you around our place these last two weeks."

Marshall wasn't surprised his grandmother took the opportunity to talk with Lovey when she had her alone. He wasn't worried, though, because he had no doubt his girl could hold her own with Grossmammi. He looked to Josh. "You asking me if I'm sweet on your sister? Because I'll tell you the truth, I'm sweet on her, all right." He ground one boot into the loose gravel in the driveway. He'd polished them that morning, giving them a good shine because it was important that a man went to church looking neat and pressed.

Caleb Gruber, whose father had hosted church, slapped his hand on his leg. "Sounds like you've got it bad, Marshall. You best watch out, otherwise you're going to find yourself a married man."

The young men all laughed again.

"You're one to talk," Marshall teased, not

in the least bit embarrassed. "It was your banns I heard read this morning. You and Mary Lewis marrying in the fall, according to the bishop." Mary, a girl from Kentucky with a sweet disposition, was living in Rose Valley with her cousins. Word was that her parents had sent her to Delaware to find a husband, and found one she had. She was a good match for Caleb, Marshall thought.

Caleb turned bright red and thrust his hands into his pants pockets, looking down.

Marshall grinned. "If you're asking my intention, Josh," he said, directing his gaze to Lovey's brother, "it's to marry Lovey, if she'll have me. This fall, same as Caleb."

"Marshall Byler!"

Marshall glanced up to see Lovey walking his way. From the look on her face beneath her big black Sunday bonnet, he could guess she'd heard what he'd said.

"If you're walking with me," she said, striding past him, her head held high, "you'd better come along."

Several of the guys snickered, but Marshall wasn't in the least bit self-conscious or annoyed. "Guess I'll see you fellows later." As he walked away, he called back, "Let me know when you want to start work, Josh. I'll be there."

Marshall and Lovey fell into step, side by side, walking across the barnyard toward the entrance to an old lane that led across the Grubers' back property, to the road he and Lovey both lived on, Persimmon Road. It was probably only a fifteen-minute walk from the Gruber house to Benjamin's place, but Marshall figured if he walked slowly, he could stretch it out to twenty minutes of private time with her. Once there, he figured if he stalled, maybe helped Benjamin feed up, he might even get an invitation to supper. Rosemary hadn't invited him to eat with them yet, but he knew it was only a matter of time. She definitely liked him, and even though she hadn't come out and said so, he thought she liked Lovey with him.

"You shouldn't say those things," Lovey told him when they were out of hearing of the men he'd been chatting with.

He glanced at her, but couldn't see her face for the shadow cast by the black bonnet. "What's that?"

She turned her head so he could get a better look at her. Her cheeks were flushed, but he didn't think it was from the July heat. "You know very well what I'm talking about."

He could tell she was trying to sound annoyed with him, but he could also tell she wasn't really all that upset. Maybe she was even flattered that he would make such a public declaration.

"That you and I are to marry," she went on. "Shame on you. I've agreed to no such thing."

Feeling bold, he reached out and grabbed her hand. "*Yet*. You haven't agreed to marry me *yet*."

They took a good five steps before she pulled her hand from his, and the minute she did, he missed it. He missed the warmth of her touch, the strength of her grip.

"Come on," he said in a playful voice. "You like me. You pretend you don't but you do."

She laughed and looked at him, then quickly looked away. Like her sisters and mother, she was dressed in black today, except for the crisp white apron she wore over her long-sleeved dress. While wearing all black to church wasn't a tradition in Kent County, apparently it had been where they'd come from. And though some women might have looked severe in the dark dress, his Lovey looked just as beautiful to him as she did in his favorite blue dress.

"Admit it," he cajoled, tapping her hand, but not being so bold again as to take it. "You're already half in love with me."

She pushed his hand away. "Behave yourself," she warned. "It's Sunday. You ought to know better."

He quickened his pace, then turned and began to walk backward in front of her along the path that was obviously well used by the Grubers and their neighbors. "I know you're coming Saturday for Sam's birthday supper, but what day can I see you before that?"

"I've got a busy week."

"Not too busy to see your beau, I hope?"

She pursed her lips but didn't correct his statement that he was her beau, which made his heart skip a beat.

"Your strap will be ready Tuesday," she told him. "If I'm working at the harness shop, I suppose you'll see me then."

"Okay, I'll be there right after morning chores on Tuesday." He continued to walk backward. "I'm taking Grossmammi to Byler's to shop on Wednesday. She wants to get a few things to make a cake for Sam. He wants a blue cake with blue icing so I sure hope they have plenty of blue food coloring. You want to ride with us? We're going to get ice cream after. You wouldn't believe how big an ice cream cone you can get at Byler's for two dollars."

She cut her eyes at him. "Why are you always trying to bribe me with ice cream?"

He opened his arms wide, enjoying their banter. "Because everyone loves ice cream!"

She shook her head as if that was foolishness. "Sam will be thirteen. That's a big birthday," she mused.

"It is, but you didn't answer my question. Want to go with us Wednesday?"

Lovey stopped suddenly, her brow creased. "Marshall, why are you doing this?" she asked.

He stood in front of her. "What?"

"This." She motioned between them. "Because…because you could have any single girl we know." She gave a nervous laugh. "Any girl in the county, according to Ginger."

"But I don't want any girl," he told her, trying to control an urge to put his arm around her shoulders. It wasn't really fitting, especially unchaperoned and, as she had pointed out, on a Sunday. He squeezed her hand tightly. "I want *you*, Lovey."

She studied him. "But *why*?"

The look on her face told him she wasn't digging for compliments the way some young women did. She honestly wanted to know why he liked her. And honestly didn't see herself the way he saw her, which he found upsetting. In his eyes, any man in the county would be blessed to have her as his wife.

"Hmm." He slipped her hand through his

arm and they fell into step side by side. "Let me see…because you're smart and—"

"I'm not smart," she interrupted.

He stopped. "*Ne*, you asked a question, now let me answer you," he chided gently.

She opened her mouth to speak, then closed it.

They were standing along the Grubers' fence line near a clump of wild Queen Anne's lace. Stepping off the path, he snapped off three white, lacy blooms and offered them to her. "For you."

She accepted them, but he could tell she was trying not to smile.

"Thank you," she whispered. Then she went on quickly, "You know these aren't native to North America. Colonists brought them here from their flower gardens in Europe and they grow like weeds now." She pressed her hand to one rosy cheek and then the other. "I don't know why I'm going on like this. You don't care about such things, flowers and such."

"Actually, I enjoy learning about anything I don't know about and I didn't know that they were once cultivated." He thought for a moment. "But they can't be weeds because I wouldn't pick weeds for you. Unless you wanted weeds," he teased.

Then Marshall tucked his hands behind his back, mostly so he wouldn't be tempted to take her hand again, and they started down the path that would lead them to her stepfather's farm. "Back to the one hundred reasons why I like you."

"There can't be a hundred," she argued.

He eyed her and she clamped her mouth shut. He went on. "You're smart and clever and witty. But not mean in your teasing." He glanced at her. "And you're kind. You're a hard worker. A faithful woman, a woman of God who strives every day to please Him. You're completely devoted to your family." He met her gaze. "But not smothering. And pretty."

"Marshall—"

"*Ne*, remember, you asked me." He waggled his finger at her. "Now let me have my say."

She gave a huff but was silent.

"You're strong-minded. Some men don't like that in a woman, but I'm used to stubborn women who say what they think. My mother was like that. And so is my grandmother." He glanced at her. "I understand she had some questions for you today?"

Lovey smiled, and when she did, her whole face lit up. "Oh, she had questions for me, all right. Among other things, she wanted to know if I could make *hasenpfeffer.*"

"Hasenpfeffer?" He laughed. "I don't even know what that is." He grimaced. "Something with *rabbit*?"

"Ya. It's a dish where you soak rabbit in vinegar for a day or so, add spices and onions and then fry it in butter." She wrinkled her nose. "I don't like it much, so I had to tell her that while I *could* cook it, it isn't something I prepare often."

"That's a good thing because I don't like rabbit."

He laughed and she laughed with him.

"I like chicken and dumplings, meat loaf, and I have to admit," he added, "I like a good *schnitz un knepp* once in a while."

"Pork and apple?" She pointed at him, using her hand that held the flowers. "*That* I can make. How do you feel about beef-and-potato pie?"

He nodded. "I like it. I also like apple pie, peach pie and especially strawberry-rhubarb pie." At the end of the fence, they made their way around a small drainage pond. "But, Lovey, I don't care what Grossmammi says, I eat just about anything. I'd eat rabbit if you made it for me."

"Well, you've no fear of that," she declared.

There was more laughter, then they fell into a comfortable silence, walking side by side, enjoying the heat of the late day sun on their faces, the call of a grackle and the hum of bees. It wasn't until they reached a three-foot-high wooden stile that went over a hedgerow of poison ivy, thorns and wild roses between the Gruber and Miller properties that Lovey spoke again.

"How did you know?" She stepped away from him, lowering her arms to her sides, the flower he had given her still in her hand.

"How did I know what?"

"Those things. What makes you think they're true?" She scrutinized him. "That day you came into Benjamin's shop, why did you ask me to ride home with you from the softball game? You couldn't have known anything about me."

Marshall took his time to respond because he understood what she meant, and he also understood that he needed to choose his words wisely. She was just starting to relax with him. He wanted to take care he didn't do anything to make her shy away from him like an untamed colt. "I can't exactly explain it, Lovey, but the minute I saw you, I knew you were the woman who was meant to be my wife." He opened his arms and let them fall.

"Maybe God led me to Benjamin's harness shop instead of Joe Troyer's that day. I don't know. I just know I was supposed to meet you. That we were supposed to walk out together. Those things about you?" He pointed at her. "I've learned those things, getting to know you." He offered a lopsided grin. "And I've asked around. Your stepbrother had nice things to say about you. He admires you."

"Who?" she demanded.

"Will. He and I have gotten to be good friends."

"Will Miller should mind his own mending." With her free hand, she grabbed a handful of the skirt of her black dress and started up the stile.

"Want some help getting over that? The rungs look wobbly," he called up to her.

"I can manage a stile just fine."

He stood back and waited his turn. "Will might have told me a few things about you, but I've been with you enough, Lovey. And I've watched you. I've seen what kind of woman you are. And you're the kind of woman I want to marry."

At the top of the stile, she turned to him and blurted, "Butter pecan." Then started down the other side.

Marshall took the first step of the stile, taking care not to touch any of the poison ivy growing on both sides of the wooden rails. "Butter pecan?" he asked. "Butter pecan what?"

"That's the kind of ice cream I want when we go to Byler's on Wednesday," she said from the other side of the hedgerow. "That's my favorite."

Marshall grinned because butter pecan was his favorite, too. "Would this be a good time to ask you again to marry me?" he called to her from the top as he watched the hem of her black dress sway as she walked away.

"No, it would not," she answered, not looking back.

But he smiled, because he could tell she was smiling, too.

"You should sit," Lovage said, taking a huge platter of fried chicken out of the basket her mother was holding. They had just arrived at Marshall's for his little brother's birthday supper, and the backyard where they would be eating was a confusion of guests arriving with baskets of food, squealing children, mothers settling babies and men unhitching their buggies.

"Put it next to the German potato salad and sourdough bread we brought," Rosemary instructed. The serving table had been set out on a screened-in back porch, which was smart, Lovage thought, because flies were bad at this time of year, especially at dusk.

"Mam, you've been tired all day. I can do this. Go sit in the chair under that nice apple tree." She pointed toward the orchard where Marshall, she presumed, had set up tables and chairs where everyone would eat. "Maybe put your feet up? One of the girls can fetch you a glass of water."

"Mind your own self, daughter," Rosemary said cheerfully, snitching a piece of crispy chicken skin that had fallen from the stoneware platter onto the table. She popped it in her mouth. "You should just get it over with and go say hello to your beau. Then you'll relax."

"I am relaxed and he's not my..." Lovage didn't finish her sentence because just talking about Marshall made her turn as red as a beet. "He's busy hosting. He has guests. A lot of guests," she said. The number of people there seemed overwhelming to Lovage. And not just from their church district, but others. There were to be sixty people coming.

"Look at all of this food," Rosemary observed, gazing over the table that was covered with a cheery gingham cloth. Besides the chicken and potato salad and bread they'd brought to share, there was roast beef, *schnitz un knepp*, corn bread, green beans, *kartoffle bolla*, mashed potato casserole, buttered beets, stewed tomatoes, gravy, English peas with dumplings, and enough gravy to swim in. And then there was the dessert table set off to the side, which featured a homemade three-layer cake frosted with bright blue, fluffy icing, and then assorted cupcakes, brownies, fruit fritters and what looked like fig pudding. It seemed as if every woman who had been invited to the birthday celebration brought her finest dish, not out of pride, but wanting to share her best with her neighbors and family. "Of course, with this many people, it takes a lot of food to feed them."

"How many people did he invite? Everyone in Kent County?" Lovage said under her breath, realizing she *was* nervous. When he had invited her and her family for Sam's birthday, she'd assumed there would be supper around his kitchen table and a slice of cake afterward. That was how her family celebrated birthdays. She had no idea it would be such a large gathering. And seeing so many people, most she didn't know, made her feel self-conscious. From the moment she got out of the buggy, she'd felt as if people were watching her. All because of Marshall's foolishness in the barnyard after church the previous weekend, she was certain. Because the Amish did like to talk, and a new couple, real or otherwise, was food for gossip among men and women. Of course, she and Marshall fell under the category of "otherwise" because they weren't even walking out.

Or were they?

"I think it's nice to have a midsummer party," Rosemary went on. "And I don't think it's *everyone* in Kent County or even Hickory Grove. Lettice and Noah from the end of our road have gone to Wisconsin to see their new granddaughters." Rosemary laughed, taking a baking powder biscuit off a plate and nibbling on it. "*Atch*, daughter, go find Marshall and say hello. You went to all that trouble finishing up your new dress." She indicated the pale blue dress Lovage had stayed up late the night before to finish. "Marshall will be pleased you wore it just for him."

Lovage wanted to protest, but her mother was right, she *had* worn it just for Marshall. Because he liked her in blue and because the blue made her feel pretty, despite her tall, thin frame and gangly arms. Because he said she was pretty.

"Let me at least get you in a chair out of the

sun," Lovage fussed, slipping their handwoven basket under the table to fetch later. "And you should put your feet up. Your ankles were swollen last night. Benjamin told me."

"Another one who should keep his thoughts to himself," her mother responded good-naturedly.

"There you are!"

Lovage froze. She already knew that voice by heart.

"*Ya*, you, Lovey. I was looking for you."

She looked over to see Marshall standing in his grandmother's petunia bed, pressing his face to the screen. He was hatless, his dark hair wavy, and he was smiling a smile that warmed her to the tips of her toes and embarrassed her at the same time. He really had no shame, talking to her that way right in front of her mother.

"How are you at playing horseshoes?" he asked. "We're getting together a game."

"She's excellent," Rosemary said. "Better than Benjamin's boys, except for Will maybe." She made her way to the screen door. "Her father taught her. My Ethan was good at horseshoes. Once won a competition at a county fair when we were young."

Lovage walked over to stand in front of Marshall, looking at him through the screen, not quite sure what to do with her hands. Just seeing him made her nervous, but also excited.

"Come on, Lovey," he coaxed, pressing his fingertips to the screen. "Show me what you're made of."

Seeing his palm, she could almost feel it against hers. She flushed. "Where's your hat?" It was unusual to see an Amish man outside without a hat. As unusual as seeing a woman without her prayer *kapp*.

"I don't know." He opened his arms wide. "I put it down somewhere. On a tree branch by the horseshoe pits. The new game's about to start. Won't you come?"

Lovage hesitated. She really wanted to play. She liked playing, but to play in front of his friends, in front of all the other young women looking for beaus, felt intimidating.

"Come on, Lovey," Marshall cajoled softly.

Lovage took a deep breath. "*Ya*, I'll play. But let me get Mam settled first."

"I've got a perfect place for her to sit. Under my Asian pear tree." He hurried to the porch door and offered his hand to Rosemary as she started down the steps. "Have you ever tasted an Asian pear, Rosemary? They're like a cross between a pear and an apple. They don't soften like pears so they store well in the root cellar. They won't be ripe until September, but I'll bring you some when they are."

When Lovage reached the top step, he offered his hand to her, as well. She met his gaze, smiled and shook her head. Helping a middle-aged woman in the family make her way down steps was one thing. What was he thinking, trying to take her hand in front of everyone in Hickory Grove?

"Can't blame a man for trying to hold a pretty girl's hand every chance he gets," he whispered to her as she reached the grass.

She shot him a look that she hoped warned him to behave himself, and then hurried to catch up with her mother. As the three of them crossed the yard, Lovage saw her neighbors watching them with interest. She put her head down, looped her arm through her mother's and followed Marshall, embarrassed, but also strangely excited. Walking behind him, she couldn't help but notice his broad shoulders and muscled arms beneath his pale blue shirt.

"You can sit right over here," Marshall told Rosemary as they entered the orchard that ran directly off his side yard. Easily covering a third of an acre, the trees were well shaped and bursting with yet-unripe fruit, the spongy grass beneath their feet freshly cut. "Look, a chair just waiting for you," he said, indicating one of two old-style webbed folding lawn chairs. "Plenty of shade here."

Lovage looked up into the tree, unable to resist her curiosity. "What have you done to the branches?" she asked, staring up at brown paper lunch sacks tied with bailing twine all over them.

"This?" He tapped one of the bags over his head. "It's how I protect the fruit. The bugs love these pears and I'm trying not to spray with chemicals if I can help it. I can't take credit, though. It was my brother's idea. See?" He tugged on one end of the string, pulled it free and then slipped the bag into his hand, revealing a green fruit about the size of a plum. "Keeps the bees and flies off the growing pears."

Lovage laughed at Sam's cleverness. And she was impressed that Marshall would let his brother convince him to try such a thing, because it certainly did look silly, three fruit trees in a diagonal line, with brown paper bags hanging from the branches. Marshall's recognition of Sam's innovation made her like him all the more.

"There he is! Come tell him what you

brought. Applesauce cake is Marshall's favorite," called a commanding, feminine voice.

Lovage looked over her shoulder to see Marshall's grandmother, the tiny Lynita Byler, practically dragging a young woman across the yard and into the orchard.

"Marshall! She's here," Lynita called to her grandson. "Faith's here. She and her parents."

Faith King, a pretty, petite blonde who looked to be between Tara's and Ginger's age was flushing with embarrassment, Lovage suspected. And Lovage was immediately sympathetic. To be put on display in front of a single man at such a public gathering had to be mortifying. Mainly since it was clear that Lynita fancied the girl in the pale pink dress as a possible match for her grandson.

"Faith. Good to see you." Marshall reached over his head to replace the paper bag over the pear he'd just shown Lovage.

"Faith made your favorite, *sohn. Blitz-kuchen.*" Lynita pushed the girl ahead of her, surprisingly strong for such a petite woman. "Tell him, Faith." She beamed at her grandson. "I had her wrap a couple of pieces of the cake and put them inside the house. In case it's all eaten before you get a slice," she explained.

Lovage looked at Faith and smiled, her

heart going out to the young girl, who had now broken out in a sweat. It was every mother's and grandmother's dream to see her children happily wed, but sometimes families pushed it too far. Lovage was instantly thankful that while Mam had expressed interested in Lovage at least considering Marshall's attention, she wasn't pushing her. "*Gudar daag*, Faith."

"*Goot* afternoon," Faith said, looking down at her small feet in pristine white canvas sneakers.

Lovage couldn't help but look down at her own feet. Size ten in black sneakers so scuffed that she could see her big toe through the threads. She pulled her foot back so it was under her skirt. This was supposed to be a casual birthday dinner; she hadn't expected the entire church district to be here. No one wore their fancy shoes. She looked at the girl's Plain, pink dress with a starched white apron over it. Or their best dress.

Then Lovage felt guilty for being so critical. It was obvious the girl wasn't comfortable with the way Lynita was touting her lightning cake. And she herself had worn a new dress. She stepped forward. "Good to see you, Lynita." She looked at Faith. "I'm

Lovage Stutzman. We said hello at church on Sunday, but we didn't get a chance to talk. I've just moved here. My mother is Rosemary Miller. Married to Benjamin, who has the new harness shop."

Faith offered a shy smile, seeming relieved to have someone to speak *to* her rather than *about* her.

"Faith's been helping her mother establish a new orchard. They lost most of their trees in that blight last year," Lynita told Marshall. "Why don't you take Faith through your orchard and show her what you're doing."

When Marshall looked down at his grandmother, he dropped the piece of string he'd been trying to use to fasten the paper bag onto the pear.

Lovage leaned over immediately and picked it up. When she held it out to him, he met her gaze. It was clear to her that Lynita wanted him to spend time alone with Faith. And it was clear Lynita favored Faith over her. Suddenly Lovage felt less confident in her budding relationship with Marshall. Faith was small and pretty and young, all the things Lovage wasn't.

"You should go," she said quietly to Marshall. And she meant it because if he wanted to be with Faith, she didn't want him here with her. But at that moment, she hoped—no, prayed—he wouldn't go.

Chapter Seven

Marshall met Lovage's green-eyed gaze and held it a moment, wondering when he had fallen in love with her. He knew it didn't make sense. He'd known her such a short time and they barely knew each other. She hadn't even agreed to walk out with him, not officially. But sometime in the last two weeks, his feelings for her had changed, gotten stronger. This revelation and the distress he saw on her face made him realize that all he wanted was to protect her and care for her. It was all he could do not to throw his arms around her and whisper in her ear that she had nothing to fear from Faith King. That they had known each other since Faith was a toddler on lead strings and that even though his grandmother might think he and Faith would make a good match, the only woman he had eyes for was Lovey.

Marshall turned to his grandmother. "Grossmammi, is that Eunice Gruber going into the house?" He pointed in the direction of the house and grimaced. "I'm sure she's just looking for a serving spoon or something, but I know how you are about people in your kitchen. About Eunice in your kitchen."

Lynita spun around so quickly that her tiny round sunglasses slid down the bridge of her nose. She puckered her mouth. "Plenty of serving spoons out on the porch. That Eunice, she better not be checking to see if I've left crumbs in my pie safe. Just because she thinks she has the cleanest kitchen in Hickory Grove, she thinks it's her business to nose in ours. She needs to mind her own mending!" With that, she strode off toward the kitchen at a remarkable speed, head down, arms pumping, prayer *kapp* strings flying behind her.

Grinning, Marshall glanced down at Faith, who looked much like a startled calf as she watched Lynita race across the green lawn. "I really am glad to see you, Faith," he said gently. "I apologize for anything my grandmother may have said to you or *will* say to you the rest of her life." He looked to Lovey. "My grandmother has been trying to arrange a marriage between us since Faith was a schoolgirl," he explained. Then he hooked his thumb in Lovey's direction. "So, you've met Lovage. Have you met her mother, Rosemary? She's a gardener, too, like you. Not just vegetables, but herbs." He leaned over and whispered in Faith's ear, "She's Jacob Miller's stepmother, you know."

Faith turned crimson and looked Rosemary's way.

Marshall had heard through Will that Faith and Jacob had spent most of the last singing at the Fishers with their heads together and that he had given her a ride home. Although, apparently, she had Jacob let her off at the end of her driveway. So her parents wouldn't know she'd ridden home with him. At twenty-two, Faith had the right in their community to spend time with whomever she pleased, within reason. But that didn't keep parents of an only child from thinking they should have more control over their daughter and her future than they did.

"It's nice to meet you." Rosemary smiled up at Faith from her seat in the lawn chair under the pear tree. She was fanning herself with a little cardboard paddle on a stick that one of the other women sitting under the trees had given her. On one side of the old-fashioned church fan was a depiction of the Lord Jesus, and on the other side, the name of a local Mennonite church. "Come sit with me a minute and tell me everything about you that I should know, Faith King." She patted the chair beside her.

Marshall flashed Rosemary a grin, guessing she knew exactly what had just transpired. He didn't know her well, but suspected she would be kind to Faith and chat with her, putting her at ease, allowing her embarrassment to fade. If she knew the gossip on Faith and her stepson, Rosemary might even arrange things so the two could bump into each other.

With Faith occupied, Marshall turned to Lovage, who was moving away from the group of women under his pear trees. "So about that walk in my orchard. Now or after we play horseshoes?"

"I didn't know we were taking a walk in your orchard."

"Well, you know now, Lovey. I've been trying my hand at grafting, and I want you to see my trees with peaches and plums on the same tree."

The most beautiful, shy smile played on her lips. "Horseshoes first. Then I imagine it will be time to eat. So if it's after dark when we take that walk, Jesse will have to go with us."

He headed toward the area on the far side

of the farmhouse where he could hear horse-shoes hitting a metal post and young men and women talking and laughing. Occasionally, one of the guys would give a hoot when he made a good throw. The whole gang of unmarried men in Hickory Grove would be there, trying to show off for their girls, or maybe hoping to impress a particular one he was sweet on.

"Need a chaperone, do we?" he asked Lovey.

"*Ya*. Where I come from, it's the way we do things. Unmarried men and women do things together in groups, or take a sibling with them. It protects everyone's reputation."

"We walked home alone together last Sunday," he pointed out.

"That was a *Sunday*," she exclaimed, as if there needed to be no further explanation.

Marshall was tempted to tease her about her naivete. Did she really think that young people who were inclined to kiss or get into worse trouble wouldn't do so on Sundays? But he decided against saying anything because she was in such a good mood, he didn't want to risk riling her. Besides, he liked her innocence. It was refreshing in a world where it was sometimes difficult to remain Plain and try to follow God's word each and every day by word and deed.

Instead, he asked, "What about once they're betrothed?" He swept off his straw hat, pushed back his hair and replaced it. "Once the banns are read, can we take a stroll through an orchard after dark?" He leaned closer, knowing he ought to behave himself and not tease her. The truth was, he would never risk her reputation or his own. He might tease, but his behavior would be nothing but acceptable to every parent in the county and their bishop, too. "How about if I promise I won't try to kiss you?"

Her face flushed. "Marshall Byler, we're not even walking out together. You keep talking like that and…"

"And what?" he said, nodding to two friends of his grandmother's who were standing in the shade of a hickory tree, their black *kapps* together, watching them, twittering like a pair of old birds on a branch.

Lovey exhaled in exasperation. "I… I…" She shook her head. "I don't know."

Then they both laughed and he wished they were alone, because then at least he could hold her hand. "Would this be a good time for me to ask you to marry me?"

"It would not." She sounded indignant. No, she sounded as if she was *trying* to sound indignant.

"Fine." He threw up his hands as he led her around the house.

"Fine what?" She looked at him suspiciously.

"Fine, when we go for our walk through my orchard, you can have your chaperone." He gestured with one hand. "Pick your chaperone. Jesse, Faith, you can even bring my grandmother if you like."

"How about Ginger?" Lovey said, her tone teasing. "She seems fond of you."

"*Ya.* Bring anyone you like. Everyone from our church district and the next." He gestured in the direction of the orchard, which was now behind him.

She was giggling as they met each other's gazes, but something in the way she looked at him made him think she was finally beginning to take him seriously.

"Mam, how many times do we have to tell you, let us do the heavy lifting," Lovage said, setting down a pair of long-handled tongs to take a wooden case of empty Ball jars from her mother's arms.

"Ya," Tara said, from where she stood at the gas stove stirring a pot of boiling water.

For the second day in a row, they were canning tomatoes from their garden, which involved an all-day process of washing the tomatoes, blanching them, peeling them, cutting them up, putting them in jars and then running them through the pressure cooker. Rosemary and four of her daughters had been working since breakfast and they still had two bushel baskets of Big Boy and Roma tomatoes to process before it was time to put out dinner for the family. The good thing was that the women had been putting up tomatoes this way since they were little and had worked out a process over the years. Stations were set up for washing the jars and sterilizing them, cleaning and blanching the tomatoes, and pouring the hot tomatoes and juices into the jars. Each woman had a job and they moved gracefully in the kitchen, working together to preserve food for the coming year.

The only one missing that morning was Nettie, and that was because she was at the harness shop completing a special order for an Englisher. Nettie, who was an artist, was painting flowers and vines with acrylic paint on a dog leash, of all things. They had all chuckled over the idea of decorating a leather leash, but also agreed that if the buyer was willing to pay for the custom work, Nettie should do it.

"Didn't Benjamin tell you this morning,

this was why the good Lord gave you daughters?" Tara asked. "So you wouldn't have to put up tomatoes by yourself."

Rosemary gave a huff, but she let Lovage take the wooden box from her. "I'll warn you. We're going to need at least two dozen more jars. They're stacked in the last room in the cellar."

"Sit," Lovage ordered, pulling a chair out from the end of the kitchen table with one bare foot. Then, realizing she sounded awfully bossy, she softened her tone. "Please, Mam. Sit and have a sip of iced tea. You've been on your feet since dawn."

"I worry about you girls," Rosemary said, lowering herself into the chair, her hand on her round belly. "If you think having a baby is an illness, your first will be hard."

Lovage decided not to bite on her mother's line of conversation. That morning, Benjamin had pulled her aside and told her he was worried that she was working too hard, not resting enough. With the August heat, he worried his Rosemary was wilting. He was also concerned for the welfare of their child, though he hadn't come out and said so directly. The Amish were funny about the way they dealt with pregnancy. It was all around them all the time. Most husbands and wives welcomed as many children as the Lord blessed them with, and families of twelve or even fifteen weren't uncommon. But it still wasn't a subject discussed between men and women, even a stepfather and his stepdaughter.

"I added ice to your tea. You should drink it. Benjamin went all the way to Byler's to get more ice this morning. His feelings will be hurt if you don't have a cold drink," Lovage said.

"I'll have a glass of tea with ice if you're pouring," Bay Laurel, Ginger's twin, volunteered as she walked out of the kitchen carrying a case of canned tomatoes, the lids still popping as they sealed. "Going down to the cellar."

"Get more jars," their mother called after her. Then she turned back to Lovage. "Fiddle," she remarked, reaching for the tall, sweaty glass in front of her. "Benjamin made the excuse of going for ice before it got too hot, but really he went for cookie dough ice cream. Those boys of his ate the last two half gallons after we went to bed last night."

"I think Jesse was eating it, too," Lovage admitted.

"This pot is ready for more tomatoes," Tara called.

"I'll get the next batch of clean ones from

the sink," Rosemary said, starting to rise from her chair.

Lovage set the jars down on the counter next to the big double farm sink and reached over to rest her hand on her mother's shoulder. "You're getting ahead of us, Mam." She chuckled, trying to make a joke of it. "And wearing us all out in this heat. Will said the thermometer down at the barn was reading ninety degrees at eleven in this morning."

Rosemary eased back into her chair and reached for a copy of *The Budget*, a national newspaper written for and by Amish and Mennonite men and women. Benjamin had been reading the current news of friends and family back in New York that morning at breakfast. The family had laughed together about the story of one of their elderly neighbors, Emma Petersheim, in the yard without her glasses, mistaking a deer on her lawn for one of her pet goats and trying to herd it back into the barn. The funniest part, they unanimously agreed, was that she had written into the paper to tell on herself.

Rosemary fanned the paper in front of her face. "Do you think someone should run more iced tea out for the men? I hate to see them working so hard in the sun on a day like this. I'm thrilled Benjamin and his boys are building me a greenhouse, but I told him it could wait until fall when this heat lets up."

Lovage tucked a lock of damp hair beneath the scarf she wore over her hair and tied at the back of her neck. They were all dressed for working in hot weather in their oldest dresses, bare feet and kerchiefs instead of prayer *kapps*. While women were expected to cover their hair with prayer *kapps* in public, at home among family and friends the rules were less strict. The same went for their state of dress. Lovage was wearing an old dress of Ginger's that was baggy and so short on her that it barely fell to her calves.

"Ginger went out to refill their glasses," Lovage told her mother. Then suddenly suspicious, she glanced at the battery-operated wall clock that looked like a shiny red apple. "But she's been gone at least twenty minutes." She picked up the considerable colander of fresh tomatoes from the food side of the sink and carried it to Tara.

Tara grabbed a big, juicy tomato from the top of the colander and eased it into the boiling water. "I know where she is," she said, glancing over Lovage's shoulder. She dropped another tomato into the pot and pointed with the long metal tongs toward the window over the kitchen sink. "Out there chatting up Marshall Byler again."

Lovage whipped around to look out the kitchen window. Sure enough, there stood Ginger, barefoot, the hem of her skirt tucked into her apron, flirting with Marshall. "I'll be right back," she said, setting the colander down on the counter beside the stove.

Tara giggled as Lovage whipped off her filthy, tomato splattered apron and tossed it over the chair beside their mother. "I was wondering how long it would take for her to upset your applecart, sister."

"No one is upsetting my applecart," Lovage said defensively. "She's supposed to be in here working with the rest of us. I know she doesn't care much for kitchen work, but fair is fair." She tucked her damp hair behind her ears and into her scarf as best she could. "I'll be right back, Mam."

Lovage passed Bay in the mudroom on her way out.

"Where are you going?" her little sister asked, a case of empty Ball jars in her arms. She spun around as Lovage whisked by.

"Ginger's flirting with Lovey's beau again!" Tara hollered from the kitchen.

"I'll be right back," Lovage told her little sister as she tried to temper her anger. This

wasn't the first time she'd caught Ginger flirting with Marshall. Only the day before, the
first day he'd come to help their stepbrothers
with the new greenhouse, she had realized
Ginger was missing from the kitchen, only
to find her down in the barnyard, watching
Marshall, shirtless, wash at the pump after a
day of hot work.

Lovage stepped out on the back lawn and
the hot, humid August heat hit her like one
of the waves she'd seen down at Rehoboth
Beach the previous weekend when she and
Marshall and several other single folks, along
with Edna and John Fisher as chaperones,
had hired a van for the day to take them to
the boardwalk. Lovage had been in awe of
the beautiful strength of the waves, and just
a little frightened by them.

She strode around the side of the house to
where thirty feet of multicolored dresses and
shirts flapped on the clothesline in the hot
wind. "Ginger!" she called. Then, through
the ripples of fabric, she caught sight of her
pretty blonde sister. Sure enough, there she
was with Lovage's beau. Well…he wasn't
officially her beau because she still hadn't
agreed to walk out with him, but her sister
certainly was aware that they were *almost* a
couple. "Ginger!" she called again.

Ginger, standing in front of Marshall, giggling, turned. The look on her face said she knew she'd been caught.

"Could you get Mam another case of quart jars from the cellar?" Lovage asked, ducking under the clothesline and making a beeline for the two of them.

Marshall looked at Lovage, smiled lazily and lifted a frosty glass of iced tea to his mouth. "There you are," he said.

Lovage strode up to them. More of Ginger's blond hair was out of her scarf than in it and the front of her pale green dress looked like it was wet, making it almost inappropriately see-through. Lovage could practically see her slip! "Mam's waiting," she said tersely.

"You came out of the house to tell me you needed a case of jars from *inside* the house?" she asked with a chuckle. Shaking her head, she looked back at Marshall. "I guess I should go inside. Let me know if you boys need more tea or anything else. We have watermelon if you're hungry." She began to walk backward from him. "Just to tide you over until dinner."

Lovage rested her hands on her hips, watching her sister go. When Ginger disappeared through the door, she turned back to Marshall.

He smiled and wiped his mouth with the back of his hand. "You shouldn't be so hard on her. She's young."

"She was flirting with you, Marshall." She tried to sound annoyed, but now that he was in her presence, she wasn't really. He did that to her. He calmed her. And made her feel more confident of his feelings for her and hers for him. Feelings she could feel growing daily. *"Again."*

He shrugged his broad shoulders. "I was wondering when you were going to come out. I thought if you didn't come soon, I was going to have to make some excuse to come up to the house."

"You would have seen me for dinner. I made tuna salad." She fussed with her hair, wishing now she'd taken a moment to run to the mirror in the bathroom and adjust her scarf. "You told me you liked tuna salad."

"I like anything you make, Lovey." He turned, dragging his boot in the bright green summer grass. "Come on, walk back with me. I don't want the guys to think I abandoned them the second day on the job."

They walked around the clothesline. "How's it going?" she asked.

"Good. Footing for the foundation is in and we're starting on the rear wall. Will made a good blueprint. He's good at planning. He already knows exactly how much lumber we're going to need and has taken into account the square footage of the old windows we're going to use." He shook his head. "It's all I can do to plan out a plot of peas in the garden. I'm fine once I get my hands into it, but I'm not one for paperwork. Or building, really." He glanced at her. "Sam's the one who's handy around our place with a hammer."

"I was wondering why you volunteered to help out with the greenhouse." She walked closer to him, the skirt of her dress brushing against his pant leg. She was amazed by how comfortable she was becoming with him. How at ease. "I can't tell you how thrilled Mam is that the boys are building it for her. She had one back in New York, and even though she would never say so, I think she misses it."

"I'm just trying to make your mother like me." He winked at her.

She laughed and gave him a little push. "She already likes you."

"Enough to tell you to marry me?"

She made a face at him. "I thought you promised not to bring up marriage for at least a week."

He pretended to be thinking, then pointed

to her. He was wearing dark denim trousers, a blue shirt, suspenders and his old straw hat with the piece missing from the brim. He looked like all the other men pitching in to build the greenhouse. Yet he didn't, not to Lovage. Because she thought he was the most handsome one among them.

"I thought I agreed to a day." He held up his finger as if thinking. "Okay, how about this. At least agree that we're walking out together."

"And why should I do that?" she teased, feeling a little giddy. Because she *was* ready to admit that she wanted to be his girl. That she practically already was, whether she would admit it or not.

"Because I'm irresistible," he explained. "And because everyone already thinks we are."

"Only because you keep telling people we are." She poked at his arm playfully.

"So that's settled." He flashed her a grin. "As far as building the greenhouse, I'm not great with a hammer, but I can do what I'm told. And I'm glad to help out." He glanced at her. "Plus, it's a chance to see you more often."

His smile was infectious. "I guess you

could have broken another *britchen* strap. You used that excuse for two weeks."

He laughed and they stopped as a speckled black-and-white Guinea hen ran in front of them. "Well, you told me it would be done in a week and then it wasn't ready. I had to come every day to check on it."

She cut her eyes at him, feeling light-hearted. Mischievous. "What makes you think it wasn't ready on time? Maybe *I* was using your *britchen* strap as a way to see *you.*"

"Ah, clever." He waggled his finger at her. "My grandmother warned me you might be one of those kinds of women. One to try to manipulate a bachelor."

"Oh." She sighed. They continued to walk side by side, past the fenced-in garden toward the sound of saws and hammers. "Is she still trying to convince you I'm not good for you?"

"*Ne*, she's coming around. *Will* come around."

Lovage caught sight of another one of her mother's Guinea hens racing across the lawn. The first she assumed was just a stray that had somehow escaped their coop, but now the second made her suspicious. "She is not," she teased. "You're just saying that to make me feel better."

"We just need to give her time." Marshall moved the glass to the other hand, glanced around and then caught Lovage's hand with his own. "Sam's already smitten with you. I think if you don't agree to marry me soon, my own brother will be moving in on my sweetheart. That was smart of you, bringing him that mechanics magazine you found at Spence's Bazaar. The way to some men's hearts is their stomach, but Sam can always be bribed with a gadget magazine or a ball of copper wire."

Lovage savored the feel of Marshall's hand in hers and felt her heart skip a beat. When she'd moved to Hickory Grove more than a month ago, she thought she knew what life had in store for her. She'd practically convinced herself she wanted to be an old maid. That it was her duty to remain at her mother's side and help her with the new ready-made family she and Benjamin had created together. But suddenly Lovage was dreaming of her own home, her own children, God willing. And of a life with Marshall.

"I didn't buy him the magazine to try to get him to like me," she argued good-heartedly. "I just saw it in a pile of old magazines for sale and thought it might be something he could get some ideas from, and it was only fifty cents. Two for—"

A third Guinea hen crossed their path, followed by a fourth and then a fifth.

"Oh, no," Lovage said, pulling her hand from Marshall's. "I bet Mam's Guineas are out again." She shook her head. "I should go."

They both stopped and stood there for a moment face-to-face, eye-to-eye. "So it's official," he said softly. "I'm your beau and you're my girl."

Lovage was just about to answer him when suddenly they were interrupted.

"Lovey!" Ginger hollered, running across the grass toward them. "Lovey, you have to come!"

The sound of her sister's voice sent a chill down Lovage's spine and she lifted her skirt and raced toward her. "What's wrong?"

"It's Mam!" Ginger shouted breathlessly. "Come quick! She's fainted!"

Chapter Eight

"I don't need to go to the hospital," Rosemary insisted, lifting the wet washcloth from her head.

From the stool beside the couch in the parlor where her mother was lying, Lovage gently replaced the cloth she'd soaked in cool water and a little eucalyptus oil. The room was relatively cool and semidark with the curtains closed, and it was quiet. Like their parlor back in New York, they rarely used the room except when they hosted church. Evenings with their new blended family, because there were thirteen of them living at the house, were usually spent in the kitchen or the larger family room, a phrase Rosemary had heard one of their English neighbors use, and now insisted that's what they call the large living room.

"Maybe just to check your blood pressure, Mam?" Lovage leaned closer, lowering her voice so that Ginger, Tara, Nettie, Bay and Jesse, who were out in the hallway where their mother couldn't see them, wouldn't hear her. "Benjamin said you told him that the midwife was concerned with your blood pressure last visit." She glanced over her shoulder at her stepfather, who was pacing the parlor liked a caged wildcat she'd once seen in a zoo. That had been her one and only trip to a zoo; she hadn't been able to bear it, seeing God's wild creatures locked up in cages, because no matter how large and airy they were, they were still cages.

"Benjamin." Rosemary made a tsking sound and turned on the couch to look at her husband. "That isn't what I said she said at all. What she *said* is that women my age can have problems with their blood pressure, and that I should get one of those fancy home blood pressure cuffs from the drugstore."

"And did you?" Lovage asked.

"*Ne*, but that has nothing to do with anything," Rosemary quipped. Then, patting her hair pinned in a bun, she cried, suddenly flustered, "Oh, my, my *kapp*! Did I—"

"Don't worry. I took it off so it wouldn't get mussed." Lovage had unpinned the starched white prayer *kapp* from her mother's barely graying red hair before they half walked, half carried her into the parlor. Once the girls had settled their mother on the couch, Lovage had placed it on a little rosewood table that had once been her maternal grandmother's. Like most women, Rosemary was very protective of her prayer *kapp*, a precious symbol of her faith. Each night, before getting into bed, Rosemary carefully removed all the straight pins that kept her *kapp* in place, removed it, stuffed it with tissue paper to keep its shape and placed it on her dresser.

"Did I wrinkle it when I fell?" she asked with concern.

Lovage smiled down at her mother. "*Ne*, not a bit, Mammi."

Rosemary sighed with relief and then glanced in Benjamin's direction. "I suppose you thought you needed to tell him," she said, not sounding all that upset about it.

"You would have wanted me to do the same if it had been Benjamin lying on the kitchen floor with tomatoes rolling all over," she teased.

Rosemary closed her eyes for a moment, resting her hands on her rounded belly. "My own fault. I should have let one of the girls move the basket of tomatoes. I just got light-headed, is all."

Smiling, Lovage glanced over her shoulder at her stepfather pacing back and forth across the room. He was hatless, his rusty brown hair plastered to his head with perspiration, except where one piece stuck up in the back like a rooster's comb. His broad, sunburned face was etched with lines of worry, his lips pressed flat together as he struggled to stay calm. Seeing him in such a state of worry brought a tenderness to Lovage's heart. He loved her mother so much that it seemed to physically pain him to see her in distress.

"Should I move the fan, Rosebud?" he asked, hurrying to adjust the direction of the big, old-fashioned metal-blade fan he'd run an extension cord to from the gas generator one of the boys had brought from the harness shop. "This better? A good thing I didn't let you talk me out of this contraption. I told you it would come in handy when I picked it up at Spence's a couple of weeks ago." He looked to Lovage. "Your mother thought it was a waste of money, an Englisher electric fan, but it moves the air around, doesn't it? Cools off the room." He stopped to stroke his gray-streaked beard thoughtfully. "Maybe I ought to get a second one, to circulate the air better in a big house like this."

"*Atch*, Benjamin, stop your fretting." Rosemary waved him away. "You're worse than a *die aldi*."

Lovage had to press her lips together and look away so as not to laugh out loud at the fact that her mother was calling her husband an old woman. Immensely relieved that it seemed her *mam* was all right, Lovage felt like she needed a good laugh.

Rosemary lifted the washcloth from her forehead again. "What are you doing in here, anyway, Benjamin?" she fussed. "A man doesn't belong in a woman's house midday. Don't you have something to do on this great big farm? Peas to hoe? A buggy to make?" She looked up at Lovage. "How long was I out?"

Lovage smiled tenderly at her mother and patiently replaced the cloth. "Just a minute, I think. You were already coming around by the time I got back to the kitchen. The girls did a good job when they realized you were going to faint. Everyone stayed calm. Tara caught you so you didn't fall and hit your head, or injure the baby." She whispered the last words in her mother's ear so as not to worry Benjamin any further. He was already distraught enough.

Rosemary closed her eyes for a moment, again exhaling. "What can I say? For the wisdom of this world is foolishness before God. Benjamin wanted to put that fan in the kitchen. He told me it was an awfully hot day for canning tomatoes. But they came ripe all at once. We certainly weren't going to let them rot on the vine. Stutzman women don't waste good food provided in abundance by the Lord."

"I told her to let me put the fan in the kitchen," Benjamin said, returning to his pacing. "I said, Rosebud, let me set that Englisher fan in the kitchen for you."

"But I hate the noise of that generator," Rosemary told him. "A person can't think with that monster rumbling!"

Lovage sat back on the stool, thinking this was the closest her mother and Benjamin had come to an argument in her presence since they'd married eighteen months ago.

"Rosebud, please let me do something for you. What can I do?" Benjamin approached the couch, wringing his beefy hands. "Could I call a driver? I can use the phone in the shop. It won't take me but a minute to run down there. I really think you *should* go to the hospital."

"Really, Benjamin, you're going to *run* to the shop. Then you'll fall, too, and what will our children do with us? We've only one couch in the parlor."

Benjamin stood over her, not seeing the humor in his wife's words. "Rosebud, please."

"I don't need to go to the hospital and that's final. What does a man know about such things? I have an appointment tomorrow with the midwife. That will be soon enough to see someone." Rosemary started to sit up. "I got overheated and closed my eyes for a moment, nothing more. I've always been a fainter, especially in the summer."

"Mam, please, lie down," Lovage insisted, "or you'll be dizzy again."

Rosemary lay back with a huff of exasperation. "Tell him, Lovey. Tell Benjamin I faint when I get hot. It has nothing to do with my *condition*."

What her mother said was true. She *did* faint in the heat sometimes when she overdid it. But when she'd been carrying Jesse, Lovage remembered, it had happened several times late in the pregnancy. And she'd been ten years younger then. "I don't disagree with him, Mam," Lovage said softly. "Let him call a driver. Just get checked out."

"And go to an Englisher hospital with all of that sickness and disease? Certainly not," she insisted, her tone becoming terse.

"Rosebud, listen to your daughter," Benjamin pleaded quietly.

Rosemary looked up at Lovage. "Could you leave us a minute, daughter. Check on the girls in the kitchen. I don't want Tara over-cooking the tomatoes. She always wants to leave them in the hot water too long. It only takes a minute or two to split the skins if the water is the proper temperature."

Lovage rose from the stool. "*Ya*, Mam. I'll see to it."

"And it's time to get dinner on the table. Past time," Rosemary fretted. "All those young men out there building my greenhouse. How ungrateful do I look, half past one and no dinner on the table?"

Lovage gently pushed Benjamin in the direction of the stool, indicating he should sit.

"Mam, I don't think the boys will mind if—"

"It's all in the icebox on the back porch. Half a ham, macaroni salad, tuna salad, sour cucumbers and watermelon pickles. Oh, and I think there's some corn salad left from yesterday. There's honey wheat bread in the bread box that Tara made yesterday. Just a simple meal."

"I'll see to it," Lovage promised.

"Three gallons of iced tea and raspberry lemonade in the icebox, too! And don't forget the blueberry pies in the pie safe. And the *ebbelkuche*! Benjamin's boys like my apple tart."

Benjamin slid onto the stool and took his wife's hand in his. "Enough now, *fraw*. Our Lovey knows how to lay out a dinner." He gazed down at her, his dark eyes filled with love. "She had the best of teachers, that one."

Lovage smiled as she backed out of the cool semidarkness of the parlor, leaving the couple to have a moment alone. Her mother was definitely feeling better, she thought as she stepped into the hall. She was giving orders again.

Lovage found Nettie, Tara and Jesse all in the hallway, standing in a cluster, whispering.

"How is she?" Tara asked, clasping her hands together anxiously. Tara was their worrier. She'd been that way since she was a toddler. She worried equally about the things that needed to be worried over and the things that didn't. Their *dat* used to say that every family needed a worrier, to take some of the burden of worrying from others.

"She's not going to the doctor?" Twenty-year-old Nettie rested her hands on her slender hips. She was still wearing her paint apron with streaks of every color of the rainbow on it. "Jacob said his father said he might be getting a driver to take her to the emergency room."

"Can I go?" Jesse asked. "Can I ride in the Englisher ambulance?"

"There will be no ambulance. Mam's fine. She's not going to the hospital." Lovage opened her arms to shoo her siblings down the hall toward the kitchen, thinking that the best thing she could do for her mother right now was get dinner on the table and then finish up the canning. "She just got overheated." She looked to her two sisters. "Where's Ginger and Bay? We need to get dinner on the table for the men working on Mam's greenhouse."

"We'll find them." Tara grabbed Nettie's hand and the girls hurried toward the kitchen, seeming thankful to have been given a task.

Lovage rested her hand on her little brother's shoulder. "Run down to the greenhouse and let the men know that dinner will be served on the back porch in fifteen minutes."

Jesse bobbed his head. "They're done working for the day. Marshall said he was going home, but said to tell him if you needed anything, if Mam needed anything, I should go fetch him."

Lovage smiled at Marshall's thoughtfulness, and a warmth washed over her as she recalled their stroll across the backyard earlier. He really was her beau!

"Oh, and he said to give you this." He slipped his hand in his pocket and pulled out a little bird nest. "He said he thought you might like it." He tilted his hand and slid it onto Lovage's open palm. "He found it in the grass in his orchard this morning."

"It's so tiny," she said, looking at the nest in her hand, truly touched by his gift. It was so small and perfect. She couldn't wait to see him again to say thank-you. Maybe she'd even walk over to his house after supper. Take Jesse with her. Pleasure curled in the pit of her stomach as she thought about how happy Marshall would be to see her for a surprise visit. Maybe they'd be able to take a walk together in his orchard. They hadn't gotten a chance the day of Sam's birthday. And maybe she'd even let him hold her hand.

A sense of guilt suddenly washed over her. Here her mother was, lying on her back on the couch midday, after a fainting spell. Her forty-five-year-old mother was in the family way and Lovey was thinking of flirting with a boy. Thinking of going to his house with the *intention* of flirting. It seemed wrong. And selfish.

"He said he knew you would like it." Jesse started down the hall and then turned back. "Oh, and he said not to forget about supper at his house Friday night. He said he hoped Mam would be feeling well enough to go, that Lynita was expecting us. We're going, right? Because I told Sam we were. He's going to show me this thing he's building so Petunia can pour herself her own grain." He laughed. "A goat feeder. Imagine that!" Her little brother turned and ran down the hallway.

"No running in the house," she called after him, wondering if maybe their family having supper with Marshall's family *wasn't* such a good idea. Maybe this wasn't a good time for the families to be getting to know each other. It wasn't uncommon for a courting couple's family to spend time together if they weren't already friends. It gave everyone a chance to get to know each other, because when a girl and a boy were courting, it was intended as a trial period before marriage. The intention of courting was to move forward to an official betrothal and then a wedding, often falling in quick succession. The Amish weren't like Englishers. They didn't date for years. They got to know each other within the confines of the rules of dating and then they made the decision as to whether or not to marry or break up.

Marshall was still asking her to marry him almost every time they were together. But what if this really wasn't the time for her to be thinking of marrying? Was her mother's fainting spell an indication that her eldest daughter needed to be here at home? Would it be selfish of her to marry and leave her mother with this huge household and a new baby?

By the time Lovage reached the kitchen, Jesse was gone. As were Tara and Nettie. There was no one else there but Benjamin's eldest son, Ethan, who would be taking over as the schoolteacher at the Hickory Grove school come September. She found him with a mop, cleaning the floor where the tomatoes had fallen when Rosemary fainted with the basket in her arms.

"Ethan, you don't have to do that."

He looked up, mop in his hand. He was a handsome man of thirty-one, tall and slender with yellow-blond hair and dark eyes. He looked like his mother, Alma, rather than his father. "I know I don't have to, but I needed something to do to feel like I was being useful to Rosemary." He shrugged. "Tara and Nettie went out to get the other girls to set the table for dinner. I told them I would finish here for them."

Lovage liked Ethan. She always had. He was soft-spoken, sincere and a man of great compassion. Three years ago, he had married and buried his wife in the same year. His Mary had been stricken with breast cancer and died on her twenty-fifth birthday. When Benjamin and Rosemary made the decision to move to Delaware, Ethan sold his own small farm and came with them, thinking he needed a new start. He didn't talk about his wife, but Lovage had a feeling he missed her deeply, so deeply that even though his father had encouraged him to start dating again, he hadn't been able to find his way there yet.

Lovage went to the cupboard and pulled out a stack of plates. "Jesse said Marshall went home?" She dared trying to sound casual.

"*Ya*, the other guys, too. They thought it best they leave us to ourselves. Let Rosemary rest. She's going to be okay, right? Tara said she'd be fine. Just got overheated. Not hard to do on a day like this."

"She'll be fine." She took down a second stack of plates. Even without the three men who had come to help with the greenhouse, Marshall, Jeb Fisher and Caleb Gruber, there would still be thirteen for the midday meal. "Probably just as well he went home," she said. "I have to see to Mam. I don't have time for Marshall's—"

"Don't do that, Lovey."

The tone of Ethan's voice made her turn to him, the stack of ironware plates in her arms. "Do what?"

"Chase him off."

"I'm not *chasing him off*," she said, prickling.

He stood to his full height of six feet, the mop looking small in his large hands. "He's a good man, Marshall Byler is."

"I know that."

"And he'd make a good husband to you, Lovey."

She felt her cheeks burn and she looked down at her bare feet. "I'm not sure this is a time for me to be courting *anyone*. Mam needs me. Today is proof of that. I should be here with her, helping her with the girls and… the work. It's a lot of work to run this house."

"What happened with Ishmael wasn't your fault, Lovey."

"I didn't say…" She frowned. "Who was talking about Ishmael? Water under the bridge."

"Don't let your chance at a good marriage with a good man—who is pretty smitten with you, I have to tell you—go because you're afraid you're not good enough for him. Because you are, Lovage. You—" His voice cracked with emotion. "You have to take the happiness you find when you find it, and enjoy every moment. Because you don't know when it will be gone."

Lovage pressed her lips together, her heart aching for her stepbrother.

"I miss her so much, Lovey. I miss her every day. And I just thank God that I was smart enough to accept the gift He gave me when He made her my wife. Even if it was for a very short time."

Lovage exhaled, her eyes tearing up. "I don't know what to say, Ethan." She hugged the plates to her. "I don't know how to ease the pain of your loss."

"You can't," he said simply. "But what you can do is accept God's gift of Marshall in your life. I'm not saying you should wed him

174 The Amish Spinster's Courtship

tomorrow, but I think you need to give him a chance. Give yourself a chance."

Ethan stood there a moment longer in silence and then walked out of the kitchen, leaving Lovage to her thoughts.

Marshall met Lovage at the back of her family's wagon. The Stutzman women had arrived in their buggy a few minutes after Benjamin and his sons and Jesse in the open wagon. The men had been given the task of transporting six pies in the back, but Lovage had taken on the task of carrying them safely into the house.

"Here, I can take two," Marshall said, holding out both hands, trying not to stare at her.

Tonight, she was in purple. Her *kapp* was neatly in place, hiding every strand of brown hair; her apron was blindingly white, and her canvas sneakers were navy blue and looked to be brand-new. Lovey's face under the white *kapp* was so full of life, so beautiful, it made his breath catch in his throat.

"We're here at last," she said, sounding a little flustered. "We had to drop Ginger off at her friend Liz's. Helping babysit while Liz's parents visit a friend in the hospital. There must have been a mix-up." She fluttered her hand. "I was sure she knew we were all coming here tonight for supper as a family."

"That's too bad Ginger couldn't make it," he said, although he was a little relieved. Ginger was a sweet enough kid, but she was making him a little uncomfortable. She seemed to go out of her way to talk to him, while she never came out and said so. What Amish girl would? He got the impression that she was hoping he would ask her out. Which made no sense to him because she knew he was walking out with her sister. Maybe it wasn't official—Lovey was just being stubborn about that. But everyone in Hickory Grove knew Lovey was his girl. She was his girl and he only had eyes for her.

"What have you got there?" He peered into the wooden boxes that had been built to carry casseroles and other various types of food. He had one himself that he and Sam had built, only they had added a slot between the chambers for hot bricks or bags of ice, depending on the type of dishes being carried to a friend or neighbor's home.

"Let's see…" She glanced at a pie that must have had three inches of meringue whipped into peaks and toasted perfectly. "Two lemon meringue…"

He groaned, gazing at the enormous pie in his hands. "I love lemon meringue pie."

"Two blueberry," she said pointing into the wooden box. "And two apple custard."

"All my favorite," he told her. "I think I'd better skip supper so I can just have pie. Which did you make?" he asked, as she handed him one of the blueberry pies, which was made with a shiny lattice top crust.

"All of them." She picked up the other blueberry pie. "I don't know where everyone's gotten to. I'll have to come back for these."

"You'll do no such thing," he said, making no effort to start for the house, because the moment they got in there, he knew they wouldn't have a minute to talk alone the remainder of the evening. They were standing face-to-face behind the wagon, only the two pies they were holding separating them. He gazed into her twinkling green eyes. "I'm really glad you and your family came tonight. You especially. I've missed you."

"Since yesterday?" she teased. Then she hesitated, as if she wanted to say something. She bit down on her lower lip. "Marshall…"

"Ya," he said quietly, the sound of her soft voice seeming louder in his ears than Jesse's and Sam's laughter coming from the barn,

and the sound of Ethan and Will talking with their father on the steps of the back porch.

"The other day when you came to work on the greenhouse. The day Mam fainted… we were joking about me being your girl and you—"

The sound of a horse and wagon coming into the barnyard made them both turn to see who it was. To Marshall's surprise he spotted Ephraim and Lois King rolling toward him, their daughter on the seat between them.

"Sorry we're late. Hope you didn't hold supper," Ephraim said, as he reined in his black Thoroughbred he'd bought at an auction close to twenty years ago. "Trying to get a wife and a daughter ready to go…" He shook his head, rolling his eyes as if Marshall knew exactly what he meant.

"Faith made two lemon meringue pies," Lois declared, barely waiting for the wagon to roll to a stop before she was over the side.

The two of them were quite a pair, with Lois near six foot tall and skinny as a bean-pole and Ephraim short and wide.

"Get your pies," Lois directed her daughter, pointing at her. Her voice seemed as sharp and bony as her finger. "Lynita said they were your favorite, Marshall, and to be sure to bring two."

Lois beamed at Marshall as if she might pounce on him. It was pretty obvious that his grandmother hadn't taken his hint the day of Sam's birthday. She still had it in her mind that he and Faith were going to walk out together. If she had her way, they'd be married by Thanksgiving. And from the look on Lois's face, he had a feeling she was of the same mind.

Marshall shifted his gaze to Lovey. She was as surprised as he was to see the Kings. And she looked uncertain, as if she still didn't quite believe he would choose her over sweet, cute little Faith. He wanted to apologize, to say he had no idea his grandmother had invited the Kings, but there was no way to say it without them hearing him. And while he would have preferred to spend the evening alone with the Miller family, getting to know them better, anyone was welcome to his table.

Lovage set her pies down and took the lemon meringue from him. "So good to see you all," she said, deftly sliding her lemon meringue pies back into the pie box in the back of her family's wagon as she greeted the Kings. "We've just arrived." She turned back to them with a big smile, handing Marshall a second blueberry pie. "So you're not late at all."

Chapter Nine

"I brought two of my rosemary roasted chickens," Lois chattered on. "Faith did most of the work, of course. She's an excellent cook, that one." She handed her daughter, who was already holding a lemon meringue pie in one hand, an enormous picnic basket with a solid wooden lid.

Even from across the driveway, Marshall could smell the chicken, which must have just come out of the oven.

"And macaroni and cheese," Lois went on. "Lynita said you love a good macaroni and cheese casserole. Faith…" She gave her daughter a nudge. "Show Marshall your pie. She makes an excellent merengue. Mile-high peaks. Better than mine, I should say."

"I didn't know they were coming," Marshall mouthed to Lovey.

Lovey pressed her lips together, looking away from him.

"We'll talk later," he whispered. *"Ya?"*

Her smile seemed forced when she made eye contact with him. *"Ya,"* she said, and then she started for the house, the apple custard pies in her hands. "Jesse!" she called to her little brother. "You and Sam see to Peaches." She indicated their white mare hitched to the wagon. "Give her a nibble of grain. There's a nose bag in the back."

"We've got grain," Marshall told her.

She didn't respond. She just kept walking, hips swaying in the lavender dress. Marshall was so mesmerized by her tall, slender form that all he could do was stand there gaping at her, the pies she had passed to him still in each hand.

"I know Lynita made a ham, but the Millers have such a big family. So many boys, I knew the chicken would be welcome." Lois was still talking as she loaded up her husband's arms with food, as well. "And grape conserve and…"

Lois was like a fly buzzing in Marshall's ear—annoying, yet harmless. "I'm sorry, what did you say, Lois?"

"I said, you like grape conserve, don't you?

Who doesn't love a hearty grape conserve, that's what I always say, don't I, Ephraim?"

"Ya," Marshall mumbled. "I like it well enough. Let me run these inside, and I'll be back out to help you carry everything else in."

"No need," Lois clucked. "We can carry it in. Faith's small, but she's strong. Got good arms on her, that one."

"There you are, Lois!" Lynita called from the screened-in back porch, waving to her neighbor. She must have just passed Lovey.

Marshall strode toward the house, eyeing his grandmother. This was no slipup, her inviting the Kings to supper on the same night he'd invited Lovey and her family, and he was more than a little exasperated with her. "Grossmammi, where do you want me to put these pies the Millers brought?"

"In the pantry." Lynita opened the screen door for him.

"Where in the pantry?" He looked down at his grandmother. "You'd best show me."

"Atch, what's gotten into you, *sohn*? You know full well—"

"Show me where you want them, Grossmammi," he repeated, holding her gaze. His tone wasn't unkind, but the look on her face told him she knew he wasn't happy with her.

His grandmother's eyes behind her wire-frame spectacles darted in the direction of the Kings, now coming up the walk in a row like ducklings. All three had their arms laden with food, with Faith bringing up the rear, her little legs pumping to keep up with her parents.

"But the Kings have just arrived—" Lynita began.

"They will find the kitchen easily enough," he told her. "They've been here before."

His grandmother puckered up her mouth until she looked like she wasn't wearing her teeth. "Fine," she declared.

Marshall walked through the large country kitchen, past the Stutzman women, who were setting out food, and directly into the pantry. The moment Marshall and his grandmother were inside the eight-by-ten room that had floor-to-ceiling wooden shelves on three sides, he set down the blueberry pies he was carrying and slid the paneled pocket door shut behind him. She took a step back from him, fussing with a row of jars of freshly canned tomato sauce on the counter.

"You invited the Kings to supper," he said. Realizing he was still wearing his straw hat, he swept it off. "Without telling me, Grossmammi. What do you have to say for yourself?"

She looked up at him, fiddling with her fingers now.

"You knew I specifically invited Lovey and her family for supper because I wanted us all to get to know each other better. Because Lovage Stutzman is the woman I intend to marry. Don't think I don't know what you're doing. Faith King is a sweet girl, but she's not for me."

Lynita tucked her hands behind her back. "Eunice Gruber said she heard that Lovage Stutzman hasn't even agreed to walk out with you. She says you're making a fool of yourself, telling everyone you're going to marry her when she's not all that interested in you." She drew herself up to her full five feet. "Eunice said she heard from her cousin that Lovage was betrothed to be married back in New York and the boy broke it off. Eunice didn't know why, and it's not our business, but you do have to wonder—"

"Let me stop you right there," Marshall said, holding up a finger. "What did our preacher say only a few weeks ago about gossip? You and Sam and I discussed the matter that Sabbath after services. Something from Ephesians, I think." He stroked his chin.

"Sohn—"

"I remember," he interrupted her. He felt bad that he was practically chastising his grandmother, but as the only adult male of the household, the faith of everyone under his roof was his responsibility. And his grandmother would certainly never hesitate to call him on such a misstep. She was the one who had taught him when he was barely off lead strings and into long pants that one of the cornerstones of their faith was their intention to strive every day to live the life God wanted them to live, not just to talk about it come each *Sunndaag.* "'Do not let any unwholesome talk come out of your mouths, but only what is helpful for building others up according to their needs, that it may benefit those who listen,'" he quoted.

Lynita looked as if she had swallowed a sour, unripe grape from the vine in the yard. "Was she?"

"Was who what?" he asked.

"Lovage." She lowered her voice. "Was she betrothed in New York?"

He looked down at the blueberry pies Lovey had brought him. And thought of the lemon meringue pies she'd left in the wagon so as not to make Faith feel bad about bringing the same pie, or, he suspected, the fact that Lovey's pie was much nicer-looking. Faith's meringue wasn't as stiff or high and looked weepy, not to mention she'd burned it just a tad. But Lovey hadn't said a word; she'd just put her pies away. No one would accuse Lovey of *hochmut*, improper pride. She was a woman who lived her faith without making a show of it like some did.

"I don't know if she was betrothed, Grossmammi," he said carefully. He could hear Lovey and her mother and her sisters talking out in the kitchen. They were discussing a quilting project the women in Hickory Grove were planning to benefit the schoolhouse. "I don't care if she was previously betrothed."

"You don't care?" Lynita questioned. "But what if she did something improper? What if she's not…suitable to be your wife, a man as upstanding in our community as you. A man who has the care of his young brother and old, feeble grandmother."

He looked down at her and scowled. And then he had to smile, because there was nothing *feeble* about Lynita Byler. "You shouldn't have invited the Kings without talking to me first about it. You and Lois's scheming, it's doing nothing but making Faith uncomfortable." He leaned over her. "Because she doesn't like me."

"*Atch!* She likes you. What young unmarried girl in Hickory Grove doesn't like you?" She threw up her tiny hands. "Any girl in the county would have you for her husband."

"But, Mammi, I don't want any girl," he said, returning his wide-brimmed hat to his head. "I want Lovage, and if you can't be happy for me, I'd ask that you at least not interfere."

"But I haven't—" His grandmother pressed her lips together.

And Marshall knew that was as close to an apology as he was going to get from her. Hearing Lois King's high-pitched voice as she touted her daughter's stitching abilities, he moved to the pantry door. "Let's plan on making our plates in the kitchen and then eating out back under the trees at the picnic tables. I need to talk to Lovey. We'll be back in ten minutes and then we can eat."

"*Sohn*. I don't think you should—"

Marshall slid open the pantry door and everyone in the kitchen went silent…as well as his grandmother. They were all looking at him, the women and Benjamin and Ephraim, when he stepped out. He strode across the big room, the heels of his boots sounding loud on the wide-plank floorboards. "Come outside with me." He walked past Lovey, grabbing her hand as he went by.

She gave a huff but allowed him to lead her out of the kitchen and across the back porch. He heard the sound of Will and his brothers in the barnyard as he led their stepsister around to the side yard, where they could have a bit of privacy. He halted in front of a purple flowering butterfly bush. He looked into her pretty green eyes. "I'm sorry." He couldn't tell now if she was amused or upset. "My grandmother. The Kings." He still clasped her hand, and surprisingly, she was letting him hold it.

"It's fine," she said. "I was just surprised to see them."

"Me, too. You probably guessed, but my grandmother invited them."

"Because she and Lois are hoping you and Faith will get together."

"Ya." He took a step closer to her. "But Grossmammi and I have had a talk."

"Ah." She smiled at him, a smile so beautiful that it made his heart swell. "We wondered what was going on in the pantry."

"I reminded her that *you* were my choice, not Faith. I don't think we'll have any more trouble with her." He took Lovey's other hand. He could hear Sam laughing. He and Jesse had gotten out a red rubber kick ball and were playing with it in the grass near the barn. "The Kings are good people. They're good neighbors. I enjoy sharing supper with them. I'm just disappointed they're here because I wanted to spend time with you and your family." He took a deep breath and let it go, letting his annoyance over the change of plans go with it. "Before the Kings came up the driveway, I think you wanted to tell me something?" He cocked his head. "About... us maybe?"

Lovey blushed and looked down, but then up at him again. *"Ya."* She said it in an exhalation. "Just that...that I'll be your girl."

He pulled his head back. "Not that you'll marry me?" he teased, pretending not to understand. "I thought you were going to tell me you want to be wed as quickly as I can make the arrangements with the bishop."

She laughed. "That's putting the cart in front of the horse, don't you think? Since you've only been my beau less than a minute." Her green eyes twinkled.

He squeezed both her hands, smiling so hard that it hurt his face. He wanted to ask her what had changed her mind, but didn't want to push her. He could be impulsive at times, but his Lovey took time to consider words before speaking them, deeds before acting on them. And he liked that in her.

She tugged on his hands, but not hard enough to break his clasp. "I'd best get back to the house, and you should probably be a good host and go talk to my brothers while we lay out supper."

"Why can't we stand here a minute longer?" he said quietly. "So I can look into your beautiful eyes." He winked at her. "I might even try to steal a kiss."

She bit down on her lower lip, suppressing a giggle. "We can't stay any longer like this because we have an audience," she whispered. Then she pulled one hand from his and pointed over his shoulder.

He turned around to see his little brother and hers standing side by side, not twenty feet from them, the red ball idle between them. Both were gawking, their eyes wide, as if they'd never seen a courting couple standing so close, holding hands.

Marshall turned back to her and they laughed together, and the sound of her laughter in his ears made him wish time would move swiftly forward, because he couldn't wait to make Lovey his wife.

It was just after breakfast, the dishes were drying in the rack, and Lovage and her sister Tara were washing eggs Tara had collected in the henhouse that morning. It was the first week of September already, but the summer heat hadn't yet broken. Benjamin's Englisher fan rattled in the far side of the kitchen. For once the house seemed quiet, though. Rosemary had gone upstairs to strip the sheets on her bed and had taken Nettie with her. Ginger and Bay were working at the harness shop. Lovage had no idea where Jesse was, but she could guess he wasn't far from Benjamin's side; the two were becoming inseparable. Their stepbrothers were all occupied in the north field cutting the summer wheat before the real heat of the day was upon them.

With the kitchen empty for once, Lovage was enjoying spending a few minutes alone with her sister. Being seven years older, Lovage never felt she was as close to Tara as their other sisters. Since she'd arrived in Hickory Grove from New York, she'd been making an effort to do household chores with her because it was a great way to better get to know her little sister, who seemed to have grown into a young woman overnight.

"My friend Sarah says you and Marshall are going to get married," Tara said to Lovage as she handed her two fresh eggs.

"I am walking out with Marshall, but I've not agreed to marry him yet," Lovage explained, feeling a flush in her cheeks. She glanced at her sister. Tara was skinny like her but shorter, so she didn't look gangly. Her eyes were green, too, but her hair was the prettiest shade of light red under her the scarf she wore. Their *mam* called it strawberry blonde. "How about you? Any boy caught your eye? You've been going to the Fishers' singings pretty regularly."

Tara shook her head, seeming emphatic. "I just go so Sarah can go. My friend Sarah Gruber. Her parents won't let her go without me. They say I'll keep her out of trouble."

Lovage set the eggs on the wet dish towel in the sink and took two more from her sister. "Is Sarah the kind of girl to get herself into trouble at a church singing?"

Tara shrugged, hesitated and then went on. "Ginger doesn't think you really like him."

"Thinks I don't like who?" Lovage picked up one of the eggs and rubbed a dirty spot with the dishrag. They never soaked eggs to clean them because the shell was semipermeable. Instead, they rinsed them off and gave them a good rub with a dishrag. If the egg was really dirty, she might spray a little watered-down vinegar on it.

It had been Bay's idea to sell extra eggs in the harness shop from their mother's hens. At first, Rosemary had thought it a silly idea. Their Amish customers all had their own eggs. But it turned out that Benjamin had enough Englisher customers that they were selling out what eggs they had every day. They were doing so well that Bay was talking about buying her own chicks come spring and raising them just to have eggs to sell.

"She says you don't really like Marshall." Tara kept her gaze fixed on the basket of eggs. "She says you're just walking out with him because he, you know...asked. And there hasn't been anyone since Ishmael," she added quickly, and then stole a peek at Lovage. "But I think she's just saying that because she's jealous. Because she liked him first."

Lovage sighed. Living with so many sisters, there was always some sort of mild drama, and she had learned a long time ago not to get worked up over things that were said. Especially when she was told something secondhand rather than receiving it directly. "I'm sure that's not it," she said, wanting to give Ginger the benefit of the doubt. "Hasn't Ginger been spending time with Sarah's big brother Thomas? They were sitting together at the school picnic Friday night."

Tara giggled. "Sarah says Thomas is definitely smitten with her. But all the boys are."

Lovage set the clean eggs on a towel on the counter to dry. "Your time will come. You'll see."

Tara shook her head. "Not me. I'm not walking out with anyone for years. How would I decide who to let court me?" she said, sounding worried. "Who to marry? It's such a big decision."

"Tara!" Nettie called. "Tara, we need help!" She sounded as if she was shouting from the top of the back staircase.

"Coming!" Tara shouted at the ceiling.

Lovage handed her a dish towel to dry her hands. "Go, I'll finish here. Don't let Mam lift those heavy baskets of laundry," she warned, as her sister hurried out of the kitchen. "You girls carry them."

Lovage started transferring more dirty eggs from the basket into the sink, gazing out the window as she went about the familiar task. She found it interesting that Ginger was telling Tara that she didn't really like Marshall. Lovage wondered if maybe Ginger *was* a little jealous, although maybe *jealous* was too strong a word. Envious perhaps. She'd always been that way. As children, if Ginger picked a butter cookie and Lovage a molasses one, halfway through her snack, Ginger would always wish she'd chosen the molasses cookie and would then spend five minutes trying to convince her big sister to give up the remainder of hers.

It had to be something akin to jealousy, because nothing had passed between Lovage and Marshall in the last three weeks that could have been interpreted as Lovage not really liking him. The truth was, the more time they spent together, the more she liked him. There was something about Marshall's easygoing attitude that gave her a confidence she'd never felt before. Not that she never questioned herself anymore, but he was making it easier for her to believe that she really *was* the things he said she was. Maybe even pretty. She smiled to herself. Pretty in a gangly kind of way.

A part of Lovage still wondered why a man like Marshall would be interested in someone like her. And sometimes at night, she lay in bed thinking of all the things that could go wrong between them. She worried he might become bored with her, because while she was trying to be more spontaneous, she was never going to be a girl like Ginger. Also, she was sticking to the guidelines of proper chaperoning. She rarely spent time completely alone with him; they almost always had other couples, Jesse, Sam or even Lynita. But what if he was looking for a fast girl? He was always teasing her about trying to kiss her, even though he hadn't actually tried. Would he be upset with her if he tried and she said no? Almost worse, what if she was so daring as to let him kiss her, and she was terrible at it?

Moving the clean eggs into a square cardboard egg carton, Lovage almost laughed aloud. Mam often teased Tara that she would go out of her way to find something to worry about. Was Lovage being just like her? Because she didn't want to be a worrywart. She wanted to enjoy her courting time with Marshall and let their relationship unfold as it may over the next few months. The fact that he was still asking her to marry him every time they were together had to be a good thing, didn't it? So maybe she needed to just relax and enjoy getting to know each other. And maybe she could even let herself start dreaming of being his wife, because suddenly it seemed that her life was full of possibilities. And all because she'd been slow to put sugar in lemonade!

Chapter Ten

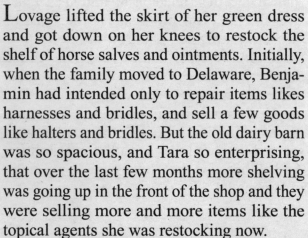

Lovage lifted the skirt of her green dress and got down on her knees to restock the shelf of horse salves and ointments. Initially, when the family moved to Delaware, Benjamin had intended only to repair items likes harnesses and bridles, and sell a few goods like halters and bridles. But the old dairy barn was so spacious, and Tara so enterprising, that over the last few months more shelving was going up in the front of the shop and they were selling more and more items like the topical agents she was restocking now.

As she opened each box, she checked the packing slip to be sure they'd received what was ordered wholesale, just the way Tara had shown her. Marking each item as accepted, she then lined up the bottles and boxes on the right shelf. Today she was restocking wound

dusting powder, antibacterial spray and a be-
tadine solution for horses and other livestock.
All the items were treatments most Amish
kept in the barn. Not that they wouldn't call
a veterinarian when they needed one. Most
families in Hickory Grove used Albert Hart-
man over at Seven Poplars. Once Mennonite,
he was now Amish. Will had explained to her
the other day, when Albert came out to have
a look at their mares, that Albert's bishop
had permitted him to continue his veterinary
work and even to drive a truck, but only during working hours. The rest of the time, he
used a horse and buggy like all the other Old
Order Amish.

"Lovey?"

She turned around to see Benjamin standing behind her, his wire-frame reading glasses
perched on the end of his nose. "Could I...
I need to speak to you about something," he
said, seeming anxious.

"Ya." She got to her feet, hoping she hadn't
made a mistake in the restocking she'd been
doing all morning.

He held a small piece of paper in his hand.
"A little bit of an awkward situation," he told
her, waving it. "I wasn't sure how to handle
it. I went up to the house and..."

Benjamin was breaking into a sweat and

Lovage couldn't help but wonder what on earth he was trying to tell her.

"Rosemary was the one who suggested I come to you," he continued.

At that moment Lovage realized that the piece of paper he was holding was a bank check.

"This came back today." He fluttered the check again. "From the bank. Insufficient funds."

"You mean it's a bad check?"

"Ya." He kept looking at her.

"So…" She frowned, feeling bad for him. "You want me to, what? Call the customer?" It seemed like an odd request from him, since it was his business. But then again, he'd just commented the previous day at the supper table about how comfortable she was with his Englisher customers and what a great addition she was to his business. His praise had made her blush and get up to refill the serving bowl of mashed potatoes even though they didn't really need them. The fact that he had such confidence in her made her feel good.

"Ne." Benjamin shifted his sturdy frame from one worn boot to the other. Then he plucked at his reddish beard that was shot through with gray. *"Ya,* I just… I'm concerned about his reputation, Lovey. This isn't

something… Not a matter to be shared outside the family."

The family? Lovage had no idea where this conversation was going. She absently swatted at a curly roll of flypaper that hung above her, precariously close to her head. The flies had been terrible all week. Everyone was hoping that the heat would soon break and cooling winds would bring more temperate days and fewer flies. She found it was taking her a bit of time to adjust to the sweltering heat of the summer here, which went well beyond summer weather in upstate New York.

"Benjamin, I'm not following."

"Marshall Byler," he finally said, speaking Marshall's name as if it pained him.

She shook her head in confusion. "I don't understand. Marshall…" Then she realized what he meant. *Marshall* had written him a bad check. She clamped her palm over her mouth in disbelief. Then put her hand out, and Benjamin passed it to her. Sure enough, Marshall's name and his house number on Persimmon Road were printed on the pale blue security check.

Lovage looked up at Benjamin. "There must be a mistake. Marshall wouldn't write you a bad check." From the look of his property, of his livestock and the clothing he and his family wore on Sunday, he seemed to be comfortable financially. He didn't seem like a man who couldn't pay his bills.

"*Ya*, that's what I thought. So I called the bank. They said the same. Insufficient funds."

She stared at the check for a moment. The first thought that went through her mind was why would Marshall have written a check for sixty-two dollars if he didn't have it? But that thought was immediately followed by a second, which was that a mistake had been made. In the time she'd known Marshall, she'd found him to be honest to the core. He would never write a check for money he didn't have. And he would never risk his reputation in the community.

"I'll take care of this," she said, reaching down to scoop up the box of products she was supposed to be stocking.

"Now?" he asked.

"*Ya.*" She pushed the box into his arms. "Now." She walked away. "Is Mam still lying down?"

"She is," he told her, watching her go.

"That's good. I'm going to take her pony cart. I'll be back shortly and then I'll finish stocking the shelves. I'll make sure Tara is here to wait on customers."

Half an hour later, Lovage rode into Marshall's barnyard. Spotting her in the pony cart, which had a bench only wide enough for two, Sam came running out of the grain shed. "Lovey." He beamed. He was now calling her Lovey, too, and she'd given up telling him that only family called her by her pet name. Maybe, secretly, she was hoping they *would* become family.

"Your brother here?" she asked, noticing their buggy wasn't in its usual spot in the carriage lean-to.

"*Ya*, in the house, I think." Sam caught the dapple-gray pony's harness and held the little gelding still while she climbed down from the cart.

"Your grandmother?"

"Gone down the road. To the Grubers. They've got relatives in from Ohio. Someone Grossmammi knew when she was a little girl. We might have to get our own supper, but Marshall said it's a good idea for a man to know how to fry up a pork chop."

Lovage couldn't help but smile at Sam. When she had first met Marshall, Sam had been so shy around her that he'd barely spoken in front her, but now he was becoming a regular chatterbox. "And how's the conveyor belt invention going?"

Sam was trying to build a conveyor belt

for a friend of Lynita's. Joe Crub from over near Marydel had recently lost a leg to diabetes and was struggling to get his chores done around his farm. One of his issues was trying to carry things like corn and grain into the barn while on crutches.

"I think I've almost got it," he told her, beaming. "Of course, it's got to be hand cranked. Joe doesn't even use propane on his farm. Says it's too fancy."

"You have to respect a man's convictions," she agreed. "Do you mind getting Taffy some water?" She pointed at the little dapple-gray pony, which was older than she was. Rosemary had brought Taffy to her marriage to her first husband, Lovage's father. "No need to unhitch her. I just need to talk to your brother for a minute."

"I'll pull her into the shed," Sam said. "Get her out of the sun." He indicated the lean-to he and Marshall had built against the barn that allowed them to pull a horse and buggy through. It was a clever design that she'd never seen before on an Amish farm.

"I won't be long." With her hand in her apron pocket, touching the check, Lovage crossed the barnyard. The barn, the outbuildings, the house and the *dawdi* house in the back were all in excellent repair, with freshly painted trim and windows that were sparkling clean. Lovage didn't think she'd ever seen a neater barnyard. Even the hard-packed dirt in front of the barn had been raked recently. The lawn was neatly mowed and someone had edged around all the buildings. Marshall had more energy than any man she'd ever met. And this was not the farm of a man who couldn't pay his bills.

She walked up the porch steps. At the kitchen door, she called through the screen. "Marshall? Hello?"

"Lovey?" he called from inside.

He appeared at the door bareheaded, grinning. "What are you doing here?" He shook his head. "That didn't come out right. I meant, what a surprise." He held the screen door open for her. "A good surprise. I wasn't expecting to see you until tonight at the softball game. You're still letting me take you and Jesse home, right?"

"*Ya.* But Jesse is going home with Adam, the boy who went for chicken and ice cream with us, so it will just be the two of us."

He raised his eyebrows. "You're going to ride home *alone* with me? Without a chaperone?" he teased.

"We'll see," she told him, following him into the kitchen.

"Sorry about the mess," he said, pointing at the kitchen table, which was covered with papers. "Trying to put together some receipts so doing my taxes next year won't be so confusing." He brought the heel of his hand to his forehead. "I've been keeping it all in grocery bags, but…"

She looked at the heaping piles of paper: checks, printed receipts, handwritten receipts on bits of paper. Her mother had always done their taxes for her father. She kept a plastic box with properly labeled files for such record keeping. It was funny that many Englishers were under the impression, for some reason, that Amish didn't pay taxes. They did. What they didn't have, which she thought sometimes was what confused Englishers, was health insurance.

He ran his hand through his hair, seeming overwhelmed, which she found interesting because she'd never seen this side of him before.

"Trying to pay some bills," he explained.

She rested her hands on her hips. "Funny you should say that, because that's why I'm here."

His forehead wrinkled. "To pay my bills?"

She shook head, staring at the mess. On the far corner of the table, she spotted a pile of checks with what appeared to be a deposit slip on top. She glanced at him as she drew the check he had written to the harness shop out of her apron pocket. "Your check wasn't good."

"What?"

She handed it to him. "You wrote this out to Benjamin's shop last week to pay for that bridle you had shortened and... I don't remember. Whatever else you had repaired."

He stared at the check. "I don't understand." He looked at her, even more flustered now. "Lovey, I have money. I'm...comfortable."

She immediately understood that he was trying to say he wasn't poor. It wasn't considered polite among her people to talk about how much money one had, not the way she sometimes heard Englishers do. Of course, the excellent state of Marshall's house and outbuildings showed that he had adequate... probably *more* than sufficient income from his farming.

"Benjamin said that the bank told him you didn't have money in your bank account."

He was still staring at the check. "Didn't have money?" He groaned. "This is embarrassing." He looked at her. "Here I am trying to convince you to marry me. Trying to convince you that I can care for you. For a family and…" He didn't finish his sentence. "Can… can I just give you cash? *Ne*, I should probably take it to Benjamin myself and apologize personally to him." He was still shaking his head. "But why isn't there any money in my account? There should be."

"What about those checks?" she asked, pointing at the pile on the corner of the table.

"What?"

"Those checks." She pointed again. "On the end of the table. That looks like a deposit slip. I used to deposit my father's paycheck for him when we would go to market on Friday. That's a deposit slip, right?"

Marshall walked over to the far side of the table and picked up the stack. "Oh, no," he groaned.

"The money you thought was in your account?" she asked.

"Ya." He looked up at her. "I wrote out the deposit slip." He rifled through the pile. "Actually three. Never went to the bank, I guess," he said sheepishly.

"Well, it's no wonder, looking at this mess. How do you keep anything straight?" She pointed at the table. "Is it okay if I have a look?"

He opened his arms. "Of course, Lovey. I don't want any secrets between us. When I marry you, what's mine will be yours."

She ignored that comment, focusing on the subject at hand. "You need a system," she told him, picking up a couple pieces of paper. She started to make piles. "And something better than a grocery bag. Whatever you spend on the farm to produce your crops is deductible, but you need the receipts. Put all those together. It helps if you have a receipts book. A way to log everything. But you still need to keep the pieces of paper." She found several bank statements, from two different banks, that didn't even look as if they'd been opened. "And you need to balance your checkbook. That way, if you think you've made a deposit and you haven't—" she continued sorting papers, going faster now "—you'll know right away. My *dat* always balanced his checkbook every Saturday morning. He showed me how it was done. I did it for him when he got sick. I can show you."

She looked up at Marshall, to find him watching her. "I'm sorry," she said, suddenly feeling self-conscious. She set down the stack of bank statements and stepped back from the table. She felt her face flush. "I overstepped." She looked down at her canvas sneakers, wishing she hadn't agreed to come today. Wishing she had just told Marshall about the check and not said anything more. "I should go," she mumbled.

"Ne." Marshall came around the table. "You didn't overstep, Lovey. I need your help." He motioned to the table and chuckled. *"Obviously* I need your help. I need you."

She looked up, meeting his gaze. "You do?"

"This is just one more example of why we're meant to be together. A marriage should be a team—that's what my *dat* always told me. That he and my *mam* were two, but they were also one. A man's and a woman's abilities should complement each other. That's what he said. My weaknesses, such as my organization—my *lack* of organization—is one of your strengths. You lack confidence in yourself sometimes." He spread his arms wide. "But I probably have too much."

He took a step closer to her and he was so near that she could feel his breath on her lips. She could feel herself falling in love with him.

"Oh, Lovey, say you'll marry me," he said softly, his voice husky.

When he said the words, it was on the tip of her tongue to say yes. Because something in her heart told her that if she didn't say yes, she would regret it the rest of her days. Something told her that for all his joking and light-heartedness, he still spoke sincerely. That he really did want to marry her.

"Let's get your finances in order," she

said softly, barely trusting her own voice. "Then we'll talk about marriage. Because if you went to speak to my mother and Benjamin right now about taking my hand in marriage—" she grimaced "—I'm not so sure they would be agreeable."

"Are you saying you'll marry me, Lovey?" He took her hand and leaned close, so close that their lips were almost touching. "Because if you don't agree to marry me, I don't know what I'll do. Because…because I've fallen in love with you."

"Just give me a little time," she whispered, mesmerized by his closeness.

Then their lips *did* touch, ever so lightly, and Lovage felt a tingling warmth pass from his mouth to hers. And she wanted to kiss him again. And again.

Then she came back to her senses. "No more of this," she whispered shakily, taking a step back, out of his arms.

Which was just in time, because Sam walked into the house. "What are you doing?" he asked.

Marshall met Lovage's gaze again and then they laughed. They laughed so hard that Sam, who had no idea what was going on, began to laugh with them.

Chapter Eleven

The first Saturday of October was bright and crisp, and the scents of autumn leaves and fresh-cut hay filled the air. Marshall and several of his friends had gathered at a farm near Rose Valley to cut hay for Caleb Gruber's grandparents. The field was a relatively small one, but Huldah and Jethro Gruber kept to the traditional ways of their childhood and wanted no automation of any sort. The hay had been cut and raked using horsepower the day before, and now the men were piling the drying hay into fragrant stacks and transferring some of it by wagon for storage in the barn.

Most men in Hickory Grove with larger farms baled their hay, or even had their English neighbors come in with tractors. They then packed the timothy and clover into huge circular bales that could be covered with weatherproof wrap so that it could be left in the field until needed. But with such a small field, the old way worked, and Marshall thought that harvesting the loose hay was a reminder of the rich past and all the wisdom that had been passed down from generation to generation.

As Jethro drove his team of gray Percherons, the men followed behind the wagon, pitching hay in and talking. Marshall had brought Sam along and his little brother was busy standing in the back of the wagon, forking hay into the center, and talking to Jethro, who seemed happy to have a companion.

As the men worked, the conversation eventually turned toward women, because that was what unmarried young Amish men liked to talk about. All unmarried young men, Amish or Englisher, Marshall suspected, liked to talk about girls. Along with Marshall and the Gruber boys, John and Caleb, Gabe and Asher Schrock, who were Caleb's grandparents' next-door neighbors, were also helping out.

"Heard the announcement was made in church a few weeks ago for your marriage to Mary Lewis," Gabe said to Caleb, lifting a forkful of hay into the wagon ahead of them. He was a short man in his twenties with a broad back and beefy hands. "You pick a day?"

Caleb grinned, lowered his head and swung his pitchfork. "First Thursday in November."

"Whoowee," Asher said, shaking his head. "Coming up awful fast. You sure you're ready to settle down?"

Caleb just kept grinning. "It is and I am. It can't happen sooner. Mary's everything I wanted in a wife—smart, pretty and she cooks a great hot *mummix*."

"I love a good hash. She have a sister?" Asher asked.

Unlike his brother, Gabe, Asher was tall and slender, taller than Marshall by half a head. Of the two brothers, Marshall liked him better. Gabe tended to be a bit mouthy, which was not a becoming trait in an Amish man. He also did this annoying thing, clicking his thumb and middle finger all the time when he talked. It was as if he always needed to be the center of attention. And he chewed tobacco. But he was only twenty-two, so Marshall was trying to cut him a little slack. Marshall suspected he'd had some bad habits as a young man of that age. Gabe would mature.

The men chuckled at the sister comment.

"Hold up!" Jethro called from the hay

wagon, and he eased his Percherons to a stop. "Got a twist workin' in the harness."

"Sam," Marshall called up. "Jump down and give Jethro a hand."

As they waited to get the operation under way again, the men gathered behind the wagon. Someone had brought an insulated gallon jug of water and they passed it around.

"I don't know why you're asking about Mary's sisters, Gabe," Caleb said. "I heard you've been walking with a girl from Seven Poplars. Elsie somebody from Wisconsin. Staying with the matchmaker?"

"Elsie? *Ne*." Gabe laughed and spat a stream of tobacco on the ground. "We're not walking out together. I've taken her home from singings a few times, but I like keeping my options open. My parents say there's no *rumspringa* here in Delaware, but I like to think I can keep my options open with that, too."

The men laughed again, but Marshall didn't join in. It wasn't that they were saying anything inappropriate. The conversation was harmless enough, and a year or two back, he probably would have laughed, as well, maybe even had something to add. But now that he had Lovey, now that he was certain she was weeks, maybe days, from agreeing to marry him, any pretty girl other than her didn't interest him. Recently, his mind had turned to more domestic thoughts, like when they would marry and if Lovey would like to travel out west for a honeymoon. Couples often did that. After marrying, they would hire drivers and spend a few weeks visiting relatives on both sides, staying in their homes. It was a way to get to know each other better without the day-to-day stresses of housework and fences that needed to be repaired. In their case, it would also be a good opportunity to spend some time alone before they joined Sam and Lynita on the farm.

"What about you, Marshall?" Asher asked, leaning on his pitchfork. "Any plans for a wedding? I heard you were walking out with that girl who just moved here from Vermont."

"New York," Marshall corrected, accepting the water jug from Caleb.

Asher frowned. "Sorry. Gabe told me she was from Vermont."

"She's Benjamin Miller's stepdaughter," Marshall said. "Benjamin has the new harness shop in Hickory Grove."

"Wait a minute!" Gabe passed his pitchfork to his brother and snapped his fingers as if trying to recall something. "She's the girl who made a bet with her sister?"

Marshall had the water jug halfway to his mouth when he stopped. He was quickly becoming annoyed with Gabe. He just wanted to finish the work here and get home. He and Sam had plans that afternoon to repair a blade on their windmill. "I don't know what you're talking about."

"Sure you do." Gabe was doing that clicking thing with his fingers again. He laughed, but it came out as more of a cackle. "The girl from Vermont or New York or wherever, she's the one who accepted the dare. Girls are like that, you know. You want to think they're not, but they are."

"Gabe." Caleb shook his head. "No gossip."

"*Ne*, this isn't gossip." Gabe stepped into the center of the circle of men, coming to stand in front of Marshall. "The sister dared her." He started the finger clicking again. "Cute thing. Ah," he groaned. "What is her name?"

Marshall took a drink from the water jug and wiped his mouth with the back of his hand. Out of the corner of his eye, he saw Sam and Jethro getting back into the wagon. "Looks like we're ready to go again."

"Ginger! That's it! I met her at Spence's one day. Pretty little thing," Gabe declared. "Her name was definitely Ginger. Ginger

Stutzman. And Elsie heard directly from Ginger, so it's not gossip, that she'd dared her sister to walk out with some guy." He shrugged. "You know. As a joke. And she did it." He cackled again and pointed. "And that was you. You're the one she went out with. Are you still dating her?"

Marshall stood there with the water jug dangling on its handle from his hand, trying to decide how to respond. A part of him felt like he needed to correct him. He didn't like the idea of anyone making up stories about the Stutzman girls. Or any young women, for that matter. But a part of him thought maybe he should just let it go, that arguing with Gabe would only egg him on.

"Gabe, don't." His brother Asher shook his head. "It's not funny."

"*Ne*, you're the one." Gabe was pointing at Marshall again. He was like an old dog that had gotten ahold of a bone. He wasn't going to let the subject drop. "What's the sister's name. Not Ginger. The other one. The one you're going out with, I guess. Got an unusual name." Yet again, he clicked his fingers.

Marshall just stood there and stared at Gabe for a minute. His annoyance was turning to anger. "You don't know what you're talking about."

"Marshall, come on. Let's get back to work." John Gruber took the water jug from him. "Gabe's like this. He likes to talk."

"Her name is Lovage," Marshall told Gabe stiffly. "I'm walking out with Lovage Stutzman."

"Well, good for you." Gabe looked at his brother and laughed, but his brother didn't laugh with him.

Marshall hesitated, debating whether or not to ask his next question. He didn't want to, but now he had to. "What dare?"

"I just told you." Gabe spat tobacco juice on the ground between them. "Ginger dared her sister to walk out with some guy from Hickory Grove."

Marshall made a show of pulling his boot back. "What do you mean, *dared*?"

"I don't know." He threw up his hands. "He…*you*, I guess…asked her out and she said no, and then her sister, the blonde, dared her to go out with you. The blonde ended up doing the sister's chores for, like, a month or something."

"Jethro's ready to go," John told the group. "Let's get the rest of this hay in before dinner. We've all got things to do at home."

"Good idea." Caleb walked past Marshall, patting him on the back as he went by. "Don't pay Gabe any mind," he said. "He's one who likes to stir up trouble. And he never gets his facts right. He probably made the whole thing up."

Marshall nodded, and took a minute to take off his hat, wipe his brow and put it square on his head again. He wanted to tell himself that Gabe had fabricated the whole story to get attention, but the fact that he knew Ginger's name and that she was a blonde and that Lovey had just come to Hickory Grove? He suddenly felt like he was falling. He saw all of his dreams tumble away. He was heartbroken and he felt like a fool. He'd told Lovey he loved her. He'd asked her to marry him. Not once, but over and over again. And all this time, she'd been silently laughing, making him the butt of her and her sister's joke. And now, thanks to Gabe, everyone in the community would know that she'd just been playing with his feelings.

"Ohh…can we have snack cakes?" Tara pointed to a display of snowball-looking cakes covered in coconut and sold in individual packaging in boxes. She turned down the next aisle of Byler's store, but was still looking back. She was pushing one cart, Nettie was pushing the other, and Lovage and her mother were loading the carts and checking items off their lists.

"We don't need snack cakes," Rosemary said absently as she scanned a section of shelves featuring spices. "I need anise, but I want the whole stars. I like to grind it myself." She rubbed her protruding abdomen as she searched. She'd been quiet all day and seemed preoccupied, but Lovage wondered if that was just normal. With only six weeks to go before the baby was born, she had to be tired, getting up at dawn every day and working until evening prayer.

Lovage grabbed a large shaker jar of cinnamon, eyeing her mother, and contemplated asking her if she was feeling all right. But she'd asked earlier in the morning and her mother's rely had been a curt "I'm *goot*." Lovage had later suggested that maybe she could take the buggy into Dover with the girls and leave her mother home to rest, but Rosemary would have none of it.

"I've been buying our groceries once a week since I married your father!" she'd declared when Lovage had tried to convince her to stay home. "An eight-pound *bobli* is not going to slow me down!"

Lovage checked the cinnamon off her list and looked for the next item. They also needed baking powder and baking soda. As she searched the next shelf, she spotted a little Englisher boy peeking at her from around the corner. He had big almond-shaped eyes and a round, flat face with a small mouth and nose. She recognized the features at once. The little boy, who looked to be about four, had Down syndrome. Back in New York, there had been a family in their church district with twins, a boy and a girl, who had it.

Lovage smiled and waved at him and his eyes grew round with surprise. Then he shyly wiggled his fingers at her. She wiggled her fingers at him.

The little boy crept around the display and stood at the end of the aisle staring at her. He had on a blue coat and a long, colorful knit stocking cap with a big pom-pom on the end that looked like something Lovage had once seen in a children's book set in Switzerland.

The little boy slowly raised his hand to his cap and then pointed at her head.

"What?" She touched her hand to her black dress bonnet. It had been chilly in the morning when they left the house. First, they'd gone to Spence's, because it was Tuesday and their *mam* had had a hankering for some pickled fish she bought at a stall there. Then they came here to Byler's, making it their last stop because ice cream was on the grocery list. They were all wearing their black cloaks and black Sunday bonnets over their prayer *kapps*. "My bonnet? You like it?"

He nodded, a little smile playing on his lips. Then he pulled off his hat and offered it to her with one hand, while pointing at her bonnet with his other hand.

Lovage laughed and her heart swelled for the little boy. She knew that some societies sometimes looked at people with a disability like this child's negatively, but among the Amish, all children were a gift from God and a blessing. Seeing the little boy made her imagine what it would be like to have a child of her own. Marshall's child. And the thought brought a mist to her eyes.

Did she love Marshall? She'd been denying it for weeks. Afraid of her feelings for him. But why should she be afraid? He'd already told her he loved her, that day at his house when they'd talked about organizing his finances.

After that day, she'd gone to his house several times, with Lynita always there, to help him put it all in order. She'd specially arranged her visits around Lynita's presence because after the kiss she and Marshall had shared, Lovage understood why parents preferred their unmarried, courting children to always have a chaperone. The feeling she had experienced when his lips had touched hers were nothing like any she'd ever had. Now she knew why Amish couples weren't encouraged to court long term. Especially at the ages she and Marshall were at. Marshall was right to push marriage at this point, because if they were committed to each other, to a Godly life, it was better that they not struggle long, fighting temptation.

"Duncan? Duncan?" a woman called from the next aisle over, sounding distraught.

Lovey walked closer to the little boy and leaned down so she was at eye level. "Is your name Duncan? Is that you?"

The little boy nodded slowly.

Lovage took his hand. "I'll be right back," she called to her sisters over her shoulder.

Tara was leaning against the cart, reading the ingredients on a box of the snowball cakes she'd somehow gotten ahold of, and their *mam* had two jars of spice in her hands, comparing the two. Lovage didn't know where Nettie had gotten to. Maybe she'd backtracked to get something their mother had forgotten. Rosemary was tiring more easily now than in the first two trimesters of her pregnancy, and even though she wouldn't admit it aloud, she was making concessions for the health of herself and the baby.

Lovage led the little English boy named Duncan to the next aisle. "Here he is," she said to a distraught-looking woman standing in the pasta section. She was wearing a baby in one of those pouches Englisher mothers liked to use and there was a toddler in the front of her grocery cart, which was so full of stuff that Lovage didn't know how she pushed it.

"Oh, Duncan, sweetie. Mama was looking everywhere for you." She leaned down to brush her son's chubby cheek with one hand, then stood. "I'm so sorry," she told Lovage. "He was here one minute and then, poof. Gone. He knows he's supposed to stay with me." She glanced at him. "Otherwise he'll have to stay home with Mom-mom, isn't that right, Duncan?"

"It's fine. It's my fault," Lovage said. "He was looking at my bonnet. I think he was trying to trade me his hat for my bonnet."

"Oh, I'm so sorry." She took the knit cap from her son's hand and pulled it down over his hair. "We don't trade hats with strangers in stores, remember, Duncan?" She smiled at Lovage. "He has this thing for hats. He *loves* hats. He has an entire storage bin at home full of them."

Often Englishers stared at the Amish. Sometimes they even pointed. Or worse, came up and asked silly questions, like the woman in a market back in New York who had asked Lovage if she watched the reality TV show about the Amish people who'd been shunned from their communities and were living in the English world. Duncan's mother either wasn't as curious about the Amish as most Englishers, or had enough sense not to behave rudely.

"You like hats, do you, Duncan?" Lovey asked him.

He nodded.

"I'm sorry. I can't give you mine, but I *can* show you another one I'm wearing. Would you like that?" she asked.

"He doesn't talk much," his mother explained softly. "But he understands everything we say."

"This is my outside bonnet. I wear it when I go to town or to church," Lovage explained. "But underneath, I wear my inside hat." She lifted her black bonnet off her head. "See?" She gently touched her prayer *kapp*. "This is what we call a *kapp*," she said, using a Pennsylvania Dutch accent.

"Isn't it pretty, Duncan?" the woman asked.

He stared wide-eyed and nodded, obviously fascinated.

"Lovey," Tara called from the next aisle. "Mam's ready to move on. I don't know where Nettie's gotten to. You'll have to push the cart. I can't push both of them."

"Coming," Lovage called. "I have to go," she told the mother. "My sister." Then she looked down at the little boy. "It was very nice to meet you, Duncan. My name's Lovey."

"Thank you," the mother said. She looked down at her son. "Tell Lovey goodbye, Duncan."

The little boy didn't speak, but he waved, and Lovage was still smiling when she went back around the corner to the next aisle. Tara was standing there alone, with both carts nearly full. It took a lot of food to feed thirteen people, especially when half of them were men.

"Mam said never mind, and for me to just stay with the carts. She's almost ready to check out but she wants you to stand in line at the deli. She says get three pounds of sliced honey ham, two pounds of sliced smoked turkey and four pounds of American cheese. Be sure to get the white kind, not the yellow."

Lovage nodded and, as she put her black

bonnet carefully back over her white *kapp*, repeated the order to her little sister.

"That's it," Tara said. "Mam said we're almost done here, so meet us at the registers."

Lovage eyed the grocery carts and spotted a box of the snowball cakes on top of one. She tapped it.

"Mam said get two boxes," her sister said defensively. "That way everyone can try one after supper tonight."

Lovage rolled her eyes and headed for the deli section. She took a paper slip with a number from the little dispenser and stepped back to get out of other customers' way. As she waited, arms crossed, she nodded at two Amish women about her age, maybe a little older, also waiting their turn at the deli counter. She didn't know them, but there were a lot of Amish families in the Dover area, and even though she'd traveled a couple times to the homes of folks outside her church district, her circle of friends and acquaintances was still small. Both Amish women had red hair and one was holding a newborn. The woman with the baby smiled and Lovage got a warm feeling as she imagined what it would be like to hold her own baby.

With nothing to do but wait her turn, she glanced at other customers waiting for service. There was so much to see that she felt like her head was spinning. Two middle-aged, blonde women were bickering loudly over someone they knew named RuPaul. One liked him and one didn't. There was a woman on her cell phone in very tight pants, wearing high-heeled boots and a green sweater that had big holes in each arm so that her shoulders were bare. Lovage felt sorry for the woman; she couldn't imagine what it would be like to stand there in line perched on those shoes and feeling cold. Standing beside Lovage, an old Englisher with big hearing aids in his ears smiled at her and she smiled back. A clerk called out another number to serve the next customer.

Turning to look behind her, to see if she could spot either of her sisters or her mother, Lovage caught sight of a man holding a gallon of milk. He was leaning over a display of bread, with his back to her, but even from the rear she knew the broad shoulders and the dark hair that stuck out from beneath the black beanie.

"Marshall!" she called, trying not to be too loud or obnoxious. She hurried over to him, a big smile on her face. She hadn't seen him since Friday. There had been talk of going visiting together on Sunday, but the plan must have fallen through because he never came by. Then she'd heard, through Will, that on Monday Marshall had hired a van and taken both Lynita and Sam to the dentist. "Marshall," she repeated, and when he didn't seem to hear her, she brazenly put her hand on his back. Right in front of everyone in the store.

Marshall whipped around. He seemed startled to see her there. "Lovage."

She smiled at him and saw at once that he looked tired. There were tiny lines around his mouth, which seemed strained. "I haven't seen you since Friday." She chuckled. "I thought we were going visiting Sunday. I guess you decided not to go?"

"I, um… Grossmammi wanted me to stop for bread. I had to go to the, um…hardware store next to Redner's grocery." He pointed in the general direction with his free hand.

She nodded, thinking that was a strange response to her asking him what happened to their Sunday plans, but maybe she'd been confused about the whole thing.

"Rye bread," he said, not sounding anything like himself. "With seeds."

"Right there." She pointed to one of the loaves. She recognized the brand because Benjamin liked rye bread with seeds. While they made a lot of bread at home, rye was time-consuming and it took different flours, so her *mam* often picked it up at the store for him.

"She's out in the buggy. Waiting," he added. "Grossmammi."

"Oh, *ya*, well, Mam and Tara and Nettie are here. I'm getting lunch meat." She pointed to the deli counter, feeling as if their conversation was rather awkward and unsure why. Was it just because they'd been seeing each other every day, and a couple days had passed without them spending time together?

He just stood there and didn't say anything.

Lovage glanced away and then back at him, feeling uneasy and not sure why, because in the last couple weeks she'd become so comfortable with him. "I guess you should go."

He started to turn away from her and she said, "Oh, are you still going to the Fishers' with me tomorrow night? Not for the actual singing. Just to help out and ride along in the hay wagons. I think we're sort of chaperones. A few weeks ago, some of the boys got into some trouble. Painted the bishop's goats with pink chalk or something." She laughed, but it was a tense laugh because his awkwardness was making her feel awkward, too. "So… we're still going?"

"Can't."

She looked at him, but he wouldn't make eye contact with her.

"Okay…" She drew out the word.

At that moment, the deli clerk called her number. She needed to go or she would lose her place in line.

"Something…came up," Marshall mumbled.

"Okay, that's fine. So…you want to come over Thursday night for supper? Some of our pumpkins are already ripe. We were thinking about carving a few before we eat. Not faces or anything, but Benjamin saw somewhere where people were carving ears of corn and such into them." She smiled. "He thought maybe we could decorate the harness shop with a few. You could bring Sam and your grandmother, too."

"I don't know." He looked away. "We'll have to see. I need to go." And with that, he walked away.

"Marshall," she called after him. "You forgot your grandmother's bread!" She picked up a loaf to take to him, but then the clerk called her number again, sounding impatient this time, and she reluctantly returned the bread to the display and hurried up to the counter.

A short time later, with pounds of lunch meat and cheese in her arms, Lovage walked to the registers at the front of the store. When she got there, she didn't see her mother or sisters, but the lines were short so she wondered if they had already paid and gone out to load the buggy. But that didn't make sense. Lovage had a little money with her, but not enough to pay for everything she'd gotten at the deli.

"There you are!" Nettie called, bursting in through the automatic doors that were marked Exit Only. "Mam says come outside right now."

"But all this lunch meat—"

"Those are our carts. Tara already spoke to a lady at customer service." She grabbed her and pulled her toward two carts that Lovage hadn't noticed when she walked up to the registers. "Just put it all in there."

"Nettie, what's going on?" Lovage opened her arms, dropping the wrapped lunch meat into one of the full carts.

Nettie grabbed her hand and pulled her toward the door. "Mam says she has to go to the hospital. She's in labor."

Chapter Twelve

There was a soft tap at the door and Lovage sat up in her chair. For a moment, she wasn't positive she had heard a knock. All she heard now was the rhythmic pulse of the heartbeat on the fetal monitor. A streetlamp outside threw a yellow glow of light through the window and across the floor and onto the hospital bed. Lovage glanced at her mother. She lay asleep, a white sheet to her chin, the blue scarf that covered her hair neatly framing her beautiful face. Benjamin, who had nodded off to sleep, too, sat upright in a chair beside Rosemary's bed. Their hands were clasped.

The knock came again.

"Come in," Lovage said softly, not wanting to wake her mother or Benjamin. He had been at her side since shortly after the ambulance had brought her to the emergency department at the local hospital. Lovage still didn't know how he'd gotten here so quickly after she called the harness shop. It was determined that her mother was in preterm labor, and she'd been admitted to the labor and delivery floor, where she had been given medication to try to stop her contractions. At thirty-four weeks, with another six to go, it was too soon for her to go into labor.

"Just wanted to see if anyone needed anything." It was Julie, Rosemary's nurse for the night. She was a short, round woman in her midfifties with white-blond hair pulled back in a ponytail. She had a voice that put everyone in her path at ease. "Some coffee? A snack? For us to leave you alone and stop asking?" She chuckled.

Lovage stood up from her chair, feeling guilty that she had dozed off for a few minutes. Her gaze flickered to the clock on the wall. It was two fifteen in the morning. "*Ne*, we don't need a thing," she answered, keeping her voice low. "Thank you. She's been asleep for nearly two hours."

"Good. That's what she needs now." The nurse walked over to look at one of the monitors Rosemary was hooked up to. One brightly lit display showed the mother's contractions, a nurse had explained to Lovage earlier in the day. The second display showed the mother's heart rate and the baby's. In this case, the *babies'*. A surprise to Lovage, but not to Rosemary and Benjamin. Apparently, they had been aware that they were having twins because she had been seeing a midwife for her care, but they had decided not to share the information with anyone.

"We keep an eye on things from the nurses' station," Julia went on. "But there have been no contractions in six hours, and Baby A and Baby B are both looking great."

"That's good, right?" Lovage asked. "If the contractions have stopped? That means the babies won't come too early?"

Julie hit a button on one of the monitors and it beeped and began to spit out a strip of paper. "Well, I can't promise you she won't go into preterm labor, but she's not going into labor tonight. The doctor will be here in the morning to talk to her and explain everything again. It's a lot to take in when it's all actually happening."

"You think she'll be able to go home tomorrow?" Lovage asked, clasping her hands. The moment the contractions had stopped, Rosemary had started fussing about wanting to go home and sleep in her own bed.

"It's not my decision, but I suspect the obstetrician on call will send her home with instructions to take it easy." Julie spoke quietly, but with an air of confidence that put Lovage at ease. "Just giving these babies another three or four weeks will make a huge difference in birth weight and lung maturity."

"I knew she was doing too much." Lovage worried aloud, glancing in her mother's direction. "There are plenty of others at home to cook and clean, but my mother likes things just so. She likes to be in control."

Julie chuckled. "Who doesn't?" She tore the strip of paper from the monitor and smoothed it between her hands. "Truthfully, it might be nothing she's done. Her age, the number of children she's had and the fact that she's carrying twins are all factors in preterm labor." She walked away from the monitor and shrugged. "No one likes to hear this, but sometimes it just happens."

She reached out and patted Lovage's arm. "Try to get some sleep. Your mother has a blood draw at five thirty, but I'll try to keep everyone out of here until then."

"Thank you so much," Lovage said, surprised by the emotion welling up in her. When they had arrived at the ED, not only had Rosemary been having contractions, but there had been some irregularity in her heartbeat. For a short time Lovage had been petrified they might lose her and the baby. Babies. But then everything had "righted itself" as her mother liked to say. Her heartbeat went back to normal and the contractions stopped. There was talk by doctors and nurses that stress had elevated her heart rate, or that there may have been a glitch in the equipment. But Lovage believed it was the prayers of her family and friends that had brought her heart back to a safe rhythm.

"You're welcome, Lovage. Please let me know if there's anything I can do for your mom or you or your family." Julie smiled. "You have a nice family. Reminds me of my own, growing up. Your stepfather was so attentive to your mother when they came in. And your brothers and sisters? I think the last of them didn't go home until midnight."

"We do have a nice family," Lovage said proudly.

Julie held her gaze for a moment in the dim light from the outside lights seeping through the window. Then she said, "Get some sleep. She's going to be fine." She took Lovage's hand, squeezed it and then walked out of the room, closing the door quietly behind her.

Lovage walked to the window and looked out at the grass a story below. She closed her eyes and murmured a silent prayer of thanks-giving for her mother's improved health and for the little babies who would soon be born into their family. Rosemary had specifically told the staff when they had done ultrasounds that she didn't want to know the sexes, but whatever the babies were, whatever their mental or physi-cal states, Lovage knew they would be loved.

Lovage opened her eyes and looked out into the darkness again. She had never been more afraid in her life than she had been today. While she'd been waiting for the doc-tors to examine her mother and to do their tests and then to treat her, Lovage had been torn between wanting to be with her mother and wanting to be with Marshall. She had been so scared and so sad, but the comfort she had longed for wasn't from her sisters or even her mother. It was Marshall she had wanted. It had been the strangest feeling. To wish she could have called him, asked him to come wait in the waiting room with her. Because once Benjamin had arrived, she'd been sent to be with her sisters and broth-ers. Waiting there for hours, she had secretly hoped that word would get to Marshall and that he would come to the hospital. Not for Rosemary, but for her. The need to be with him had almost been overwhelming.

And that was when Lovage realized she had fallen in love with Marshall.

She didn't know when it had happened or how. She had never been in love, but in her heart, she knew that the feelings rushing through her right now were not the physical desire she had felt for him that day they had kissed, but a genuine love. A love that would be the makings of a solid, happy marriage. Not that she didn't think there would be bumps along the road, but if Marshall possessed half the love for her that she felt for him, she knew they could have a faithful, honorable, loving life together. And he had told her he loved her. He'd told her the day they had kissed and had told her every time they'd said goodbye since then.

Just thinking about it sent a shiver down her spine, as if she were cold, but also as if she were warm. She smiled and saw her reflection in the window glass: angular face, wide-set eyes, high cheekbones, a small nose, small chin and wisps of brown hair that had fallen from her *kapp*. She had never thought she was beautiful. How could she have when she was so tall and skinny and browned-haired like a wren, and surrounded by the red-haired, oval-faced loveliness of her mother and sisters? But looking at her own reflection tonight, she smiled. Because Marshall had said she was beautiful. And that made her feel beautiful.

"Lovey..." Rosemary called, sleepily.

Lovage spun around and then rushed to her mother's bedside. "Mam? How are you feeling?"

"Shh," Rosemary whispered. She pointed to Benjamin. "He needs his sleep."

"Ya," she murmured, pulling her chair closer to the side of the bed. "But you should be asleep, too."

"Nonsense." Mam glanced at the clock on the wall. "I've slept most of the day and all of the night away." She reached for her daughter's hand. "Where are the other girls? Not still in the waiting room, I pray."

"Ne. Ethan sent them all home around eight. Jesse, too. And the boys. Only he and Will stayed. To be sure you or their father didn't need anything. I think they left around midnight."

"They're good boys," she mused. "I'm glad everyone went home." She squeezed Lovage's hand. "You should have gone, too, *dochtah.*"

"I thought maybe Benjamin—" Thinking better of her words, Lovage didn't finish her sentence.

What she had intended to say was that she had stayed thinking Benjamin would go home. But she realized she'd been foolish to ever believe that. Because she had been blind to the relationship her mother and Benjamin had. And now, suddenly, she understood it. Her feelings for Marshall made her realize that the bond between Benjamin and her *mam*, the love between them, was about togetherness, not separation during times of trial. The thought made her sad that she hadn't seen it sooner, that she hadn't listened to her mother when Rosemary had tried to tell her. But she also felt hopeful that she and Marshall could share that same kind of love.

Lovage looked down at her mother and smiled. "*Ya*, I probably should have gone home, but it's too late now. Ethan said he would be back in the morning."

"I'm sorry I caused such a fuss." She shook her head. "Really, an ambulance. And *atch*!" Her hands flew to her head. "All those groceries, so much for those girls at Byler's to put back on the shelves."

"Not to worry," Lovage told her. "Will went by Byler's, paid for it all with cash from the household money jar, and Eunice and Barnabas took their wagon and fetched it. Eunice came to the waiting room later. She said to tell you it was all put away properly." She chuckled, remembering the conversation that had taken place while they stood in front of a big machine full of snacks in a cubby in the waiting room. Lovage had been so hungry at that point that she had seriously thought about getting herself a bag of pretzels and a candy bar. "And she also said to tell you that you buy too much ice cream and that will make you fat." She looked quizzically down at her mother. "She said you would know what she meant?"

Rosemary laughed. "It's a joke we have." She rested her hand on her big belly. "That we're fat because of what we've been eating and not for the real reason."

Lovage looked away, feeling the heat of embarrassment on her cheeks. But also, deep down, she was pleased her mother would share such an intimate little joke with her. As if they were friends and not mother and daughter. And she couldn't help wondering if the change had something to do with her feelings for Marshall. Did her *mam* know?

Lovage looked at her and said softly, "I'm glad you and the babies are all right. I didn't tell anyone, not even Ginger, that there are two babies."

"I hope you don't mind that I didn't say. The midwife heard the two heartbeats months ago, but Benjamin and I talked and—" she hesitated "—we decided not to say anything, not because we were afraid something might happen, but because we wanted to just have a little secret between ourselves. That may be hard for you to understand, but sometimes a couple—"

"*Ne*, I do understand." Lovage smiled, thinking about the revelation she had experienced tonight in regards to her feelings for Marshall. And now she just wanted to see him, to be with him so she could tell him. And so that the next time he asked her to marry him, which seemed to happen nearly every time they were together, she could say yes. She could agree to be his wife. "I think I understand now that…" She looked away, feeling a little shy. "Since Marshall and I have…"

"Fallen in love?" Rosemary asked, with a mixture of amusement and happiness in her voice.

Lovage made herself look at her mother. "*Ya*, I think… I *know* I love him." And then for the first time all day, she remembered her exchange with him in Byler's. She frowned. "I didn't get to tell you. I saw him at Byler's when I was getting the meat from the deli." She shook her head slowly, thinking it felt like such a long time ago. "We just spoke for a minute but...he said he couldn't go to the singing tonight with me. We were supposed to chaperone."

"Something came up?" Rosemary reached for a plastic cup of water on a table beside the bed.

"*Ya*... I suppose." Thinking back, Lovage met her mother's gaze. She was a little concerned now. Because his behavior had been so odd. "I'm not sure. He was in a hurry. Lynita was waiting in the parking lot, but... He didn't really say why he couldn't go tonight or why he hadn't come for me Sunday. Remember? I thought we were going visiting?"

"It's probably nothing," Rosemary assured her, taking a sip of her water. "It's harvest time. There's a lot of work to be done to get the house and farm and livestock ready for winter. Benjamin has been preoccupied, as well."

"*Ya*, I'm sure he'll come by the house tomorrow. When he hears I've been here all night with you." Lovage sat back in her chair. "I'm sure it's nothing," she agreed, despite a sudden niggling feeling that maybe something *was* amiss.

"Toby," Marshall said impatiently. "Hold still, boy!" Standing in his barnyard, he lifted the horse's hoof again and rested it against his knee. The young gelding had seemed a little lame this morning when he and Sam had gone to the feed store with the wagon. They had gone to get a couple hundred pounds of horse, cow and goat chow that he would use in the coming winter to supplement the corn and hay he was harvesting from his fields now.

Marshall suspected that Toby had picked up a stone along the way, but now, looking at the horse's hoof, he thought otherwise. He was immediately annoyed. "Sam, did you clean Toby's hooves this morning before harnessing him?"

Sam was playing with his brown-and-white goat, Petunia. He'd fashioned a blanket with pockets on each side from two burlap feed bags and was trying to tie it on the less-than-cooperative animal. "*Ya*, I cleaned his hooves."

"Not well enough. Look at this." He tapped Toby's horseshoe and then used the hoof pick in his hand to point out a tiny pebble wedged between the frog—the V-shaped inner part—and the wall of the hoof. The soft flesh around the pebble was slightly swollen, indicating it had been there longer than an hour or so.

"This could have seriously injured the horse, Sam," he said sharply.

His brother stared at the hoof. "I... I'm sorry. I must have missed it."

"When you tell me you've done something, I expect you to be truthful with me."

"I *am* being truthful." Sam's voice quavered. "I cleaned his hooves, but I guess I missed that little rock. I'm sorry."

"Do it correctly next time." Marshall popped out the rock and then exchanged the pick for a hoof brush from his back pocket. "Pigs watered?"

"*Ne,* but I'll do it now," Sam said, backing away from him.

"And put that goat up," Marshall called. "We have work to be done today. If you want to do a man's work, you shouldn't be wasting daylight playing with a pet."

The moment the words came out of his mouth, Marshall regretted them. Maybe not the words. It was his job to teach Sam how to care for animals, how to run a farm. But he regretted the tone he had used with his little brother. But he didn't stop Sam to apologize then; he let him go. He would do it later.

Marshall had been in a foul mood all morning. Actually, for days. Long enough for both his grandmother and brother to notice. And she was so perceptive that she had figured out almost immediately who he was upset with, and had been asking questions.

"Haven't seen Lovage in a few days," she had commented that morning at breakfast. She'd made French toast, link sausages with maple syrup and freshly baked buttermilk biscuits with hot apple butter to slather them with.

"Bloom off the rose?" his *grossmammi* had pressed.

"I don't want to talk about," he'd responded.

"I hear Rosemary's home from the hospital. I was thinking I would pay a visit this afternoon. I made an apple cake. You want to go with me?"

Marshall had shaken his head and forked a large square of French toast into his mouth. "*Ne*, too much to do around here today. We need grain and I need to disk up part of the garden, but I've got a bent blade that needs to be repaired. I don't know how a disk blade gets bent," he grumbled. "We've got no rocks in our soil."

His grandmother had opened her mouth as if wanting to speak again, then closed it and refreshed his coffee.

Finishing Toby's last hoof, Marshall grabbed the halter and led the horse back around to the pasture gate. He slipped off the nylon halter and gave the gelding a pat on its haunch as he set it free. He closed the gate, but then just stood there, gazing out at the pasture.

The sun was shining and there was a light breeze coming out of the west, carrying the scent of the last of his ripe apples. Only he could barely feel the warmth on his face. He couldn't appreciate the sweet, sharp scents of fall.

Because he was miserable.

How could everything have gone so wrong with Lovey? How could he have been such a fool? He had known in the beginning, when he'd first met her at the harness shop, that she'd not really be interested in him. But then she had seemed to take a liking to him. And she'd continued to agree to go out with him. She'd let him ask her to marry him again and again. She'd stood there and let him tell her he was in love with her. And now he knew that it had all been a game to her. Fun between two sisters.

Marshall groaned and rested his back against the gate. He didn't know what to do. He'd been so upset Tuesday when he'd seen her at Byler's that he'd barely been able to speak to her. He knew he should confront her and make her confess that the only reason she'd been going out with him was because of some silly dare Ginger had made. But would she even admit it? And what would be the point? She didn't love him. She was never going to love him.

He closed his eyes, wishing he had someone to talk about this with. Someone who could give him advice. But who could he talk to? His grandmother had been set against Lovey from the beginning. And his best friend, Will, was Lovey's stepbrother.

With a sigh, Marshall headed for the barn. Right now, the best thing he could think to do was work. Hard work tired a man's muscles and made him sleep at night. It kept him from thinking too long on the love that had almost been.

Chapter Thirteen

Lovage stood near the Fishers' farmhouse, listening to the neighborhood women speak softly in Pennsylvania *Deutsch* as they loaded children into their buggies to go home. It had been a long day of church services. They'd had a guest preacher, Bishop Simon from Ohio, and he had been so long-winded that parishioners had to be gently poked to wake them during the second service. Both the morning and afternoon sermons had been related to mercy, but Lovage had to admit, though she refrained from falling asleep, she'd not been in a good frame of mind to hear and digest God's word.

A fierce wind coming out of the north tugged at the hem of her heavy wool cloak and pulled at the strings of her black bonnet. It was a cold, late afternoon with black skies, but she had decided to walk home rather than ride with her family, to give herself some time to think.

About Marshall. About what she should do about him.

For a day or two following her mother's release from the hospital, Lovage had told herself that Marshall hadn't come around because he didn't want to bother the family. It made sense he might think that, considering the circumstances, Rosemary's household needed as little commotion as possible. Maybe he'd even been embarrassed, because his grandmother must have told him why Rosemary had been hospitalized, and pregnancy was not something discussed among Amish men. But when Lynita had stopped by to visit Rosemary, she had sounded as if she was making excuses as to why her grandson hadn't come with her. Something about a plow blade being broken. Fall chores to be done. A sagging shutter. But then another day had passed. Then another. And today, while Marshall had been present for the district church services, he had openly avoided Lovage. Not only had he kept away from her during the services and the midday meal, but he'd refused to make eye contact with her, even from across a room.

Lovage was heartbroken. She couldn't possibly imagine how he could have seemed so in love with her less than two weeks ago, how he could have asked her to marry him yet again, and now he couldn't even look at her. Had she done something, *said* something, to upset him? Or worse, had he realized how dull she was? Had he decided he really did want someone fun to be his wife?

A buggy rolled by and three-year-old Elsa Gruber waved excitedly from the open rear window. Lovage waved back with one cold hand, wishing she'd worn her wool knit gloves. In this wind, her hands would be near frozen by the time she got home. The sight of little Elsa's face as the buggy went down the driveway brought a lump up in Lovage's throat. What if Marshall didn't love her anymore? Didn't want to marry her? If this was over, could she ever find love again? Because seeing Benjamin and her mother together in the hospital had made her realize that she really had done the right thing when she had refused Ishmael's marriage proposal. Because she knew what a marriage of love looked like. And she wasn't going to settle for less. Amish couples didn't always marry for love. There were various alternative reasons, such as arranged matches or security for a widow. But Lovage wanted what Benjamin and her mother had. What her parents had had.

Tugging on the brim of her bonnet to shield her face from the wind, she started across the barnyard. There was a gathering of older men near the smokehouse, their heads bowed, the brims of their black hats almost touching as they engaged in conversation with the visiting preacher. Bishop Simon saw her and nodded, then returned his attention to the group. That was when she spotted Marshall hitching Toby to his grandmother's buggy.

She halted, the wind in her face, watching him. His head was down, and a knit watch cap had replaced his black Sunday church hat. His shoulders were hunched inside a black wool coat and he seemed to be moving in slow motion. She stood there for a moment in indecision. If he'd changed his mind and didn't love her anymore, did the reason matter? Should she just let it go and not subject either of them to the awkwardness of him having to say why he didn't want to marry her anymore? Or should she confront him?

After another moment of uncertainty, she strode across the barnyard. She waited until she was right behind him to speak his name.

He didn't hear her approach, maybe because of the howling wind.

"Marshall?" she said to his back a second time.

He hesitated before he turned around, almost as if debating whether or not to acknowledge her.

Lovage's heart fell further.

"Marshall, I have to talk to you." Tears burned behind her eyelids and a part of her wanted to turn and run. But Rosemary hadn't raised her to be a coward. And wouldn't it be better to know why he didn't love her anymore than to never know? "I need you to tell me what's happened," she managed to say when she found her voice again. "Between us. Last I knew, all was well. You asked me to marry you two weeks ago at Chupps' barn raising and then…then you didn't come for me last Sunday and I saw you at Byler's and you acted strange." She lifted her arms and let them fall to her sides. She was shivering, but she wasn't sure if it was because she was cold or because she was so upset. "What changed?"

He didn't make eye contact with her and her resolve wavered. Maybe it would be best if she turned around and walked away. But she deserved better. If he didn't love her anymore, he needed to say so. And he needed to tell her why. If he was going to break her heart, she deserved an explanation.

She waited, but he was silent.

"Marshall, say something," she said finally. "Anything."

He ran his hand along one of the thick straps of his horse's harness. "You know very well why I'm upset." His voice was harsh and angry, a tone she'd never heard from him in the three months she had known him.

"*Ne*, I don't," she said softly. "At the barn raising everything was fine." She gave a strangled little laugh. "You told me—" Her voice caught in her throat. "That you loved me," she finished in a great exhalation.

Marshall slowly lifted his gaze until he was eye-to-eye with her. "You know why," he repeated, harsh accusation in his voice. Pain. "Everyone knows."

"Knows *what*?" she demanded, raising her voice to him. "Marshall, how can I explain myself to you, defend myself, if you don't tell me why you're upset with me?"

"I felt like a fool when I heard, Lovage. Everyone in Hickory Grove and Rose Valley knew and I didn't. The joke was on me, wasn't it?"

"Marshall, you have to believe me when I say I don't know what you're talking about." She hesitated, racking her brain, but still could think of nothing she had done. "What did you hear? I have a right to know."

"I'm not a playing piece in a game of checkers, you know. My intentions were honest and honorable from the first day I met you. From that first day, I meant every word I said. Lovey, I—" His voice cracked and he went silent.

"Marshall," she begged, making fists of her hands. "Please tell me what we're talking about."

"The dare," he told her.

She held his gaze for an instant, truly having no idea what he was talking about.

And then she knew. And she was crestfallen.

It seemed as if it had been so long ago and so...*trivial* to her. Silliness between sisters. Ginger had genuinely wanted Lovage to get out and make new friends, perhaps even find a beau. "The dare," she murmured. Wind tugged at the skirt of her black dress. "Ginger's dare."

Marshall turned and stroked Toby's flank. "Ginger's dare."

"So Ginger told you," she said. It was a statement, not a question.

"*Ne*, worse than that." His voiced sounded flat now, which seemed worse than his anger. "She told others. Everyone is talking about it. Guys in Rose Valley knew. Everyone is laughing about it. Laughing at *me*."

She closed her eyes for a moment. The sun was setting fast. Soon it wouldn't be safe for her to walk home along the road because she'd brought no flashlight with her. And her family had already left in their buggies.

"Marshall," she said. "It's true that Ginger *did* dare me to ride home from the softball game with you, but…" She exhaled and started again. "I accepted her dare, but it was all in good fun. And you have to believe me when I tell you that after that, I walked out with you because I wanted to. Because I *wanted* to be with you."

"She did your chores for a month, so was that the deal? That you would walk out with me for a month?" he asked. "What did she offer you for the next month?"

She almost laughed, his accusation seemed so ridiculous, but she knew from the look on his face, from the tone of his voice, that he didn't think it was ridiculous. "It was dishes and it was only for a week. One ride home with you and Ginger said she'd take on my dishwashing chore for a week. I'm sorry. I should have told you after that first date." She clasped her hands together, almost as if begging him. "It was wrong of me not to tell you, Marshall. But I have to be honest with you, I didn't take you entirely seriously at first. When you started asking me to go places with you. Who asks a woman to marry her on their first date?"

"I'm sorry. I have to go. My grandmother and brother are waiting out front for me to pick them up." He stepped between her and the buggy and swung up into the seat.

"Marshall, what are you doing? That's it?" She opened her arms to him, looking up at him on the buggy seat. "You're not going to talk with me about this?"

"Nothing to talk about." He slid the door shut, lifted the reins and urged Toby forward.

Lovage stood there in the cold, fighting tears until he was gone. Then she walked home alone in the dark.

When Lovage walked into her mother's kitchen, Rosemary was sitting at the table with Benjamin, both with cups of tea. He was reading aloud to her from the Book of Ruth, Rosemary's favorite. He glanced over the top of the newspaper at his stepdaughter, his wire-frame reading glasses perched on the end of his large nose. "Have a good walk home, Lovey?"

"Ya," she answered. "It was cold, but the exercise felt good after sitting so long today." She'd removed her cloak in the laundry room and left it there. She now took off her bonnet and added it to the row of her sisters' and Mam's on a shelf inside the kitchen door.

Rosemary was sewing a button on one of the boys' shirts. Technically, there was supposed to be no work done on the Sabbath, but Benjamin was lax in some regards. In a household so large, there was so much to do. Mending seemed a minor infraction, especially while listening to a reading from the Bible.

"Did you speak with him?" her *mam* asked. If she could tell that Lovage had been crying on the walk home, she didn't say.

Lovage pressed her lips together. Her mother was aware that something was going on between her and Marshall, but she didn't understand how serious it was because Lovage didn't want her to know. Her mother didn't need the worry. *"Ya.* Do you know where Ginger is?"

"Gone upstairs, I think. Looking for her

favorite shampoo. She seems to believe that Nettie borrowed it, but they disagree." Rosemary held her gaze a moment longer, seeming to debate whether to press her any further on the subject of Marshall, but then let it go and returned her attention to the errant button. "We'll begin putting supper on in a half hour. The boys are out milking and feeding."

"*Ya*, I'll be right back down. The stew left on the woodstove all day will be easy to serve," Lovage said, crossing the kitchen, which smelled deliciously of roasting beef and hearty vegetables. "And there's still plenty of corn bread and cinnamon applesauce and two huge dishes of blueberry crisp that Nettie made yesterday."

Benjamin waited until Lovage left the kitchen and began reading aloud again.

Lovage took the stairs two at time. "Ginger?" she called from the landing at the top.

"In the bathroom!" her sister called back. "I can't find my shampoo in the gold bottle. The one that smells like almonds," she went on. "Do you know where it is? Nettie says she put it back, but I can't find it anywhere."

Lovage stepped into the large family bathroom to find Ginger, still in her black *karrichdaag* dress, on her hands and knees on the floor, her head thrust under the sink. The airy room was painted a buttercup yellow with white trim and smelled of dried herbs and fresh linens hung to dry in the outdoors.

"*Ne*, I've not seen it." Lovage closed the door, because she didn't want anyone else to hear them.

"I know Nettie used it. I hope it's not all gone. I bought that shampoo with my own money..." Ginger chattered on.

Lovage crossed her arms over her chest, still feeling chilled from her walk, though the house was warm. "I don't think I'll be seeing Marshall anymore," she said, her voice sounding strained.

"Oh, Lovey." Ginger came out from under the sink and looked up at her. "I'm so sorry. But it's better that you decide you're not like-minded now, than after you're married, *ya*?"

Lovage shook her head slowly, trying to fight the anger that was abruptly bubbling up inside her. She tamped it down. "I hadn't even agreed to marry him. But I was going to, because I've fallen in love with him," she said evenly, when she had found her voice again. "But now it's too late, because he found out about the dare. About you daring me to ride home with him that first night. And he's furious. He thinks the only reason I've been seeing him is because of the dare. And..." Tears unexpectedly filled her eyes. "And I think he's broken my heart."

"Oh, Lovey." Ginger stared up at her for a long moment, and then got to her feet, tears springing into her own eyes. "I didn't know... I didn't realize you cared for him that way."

Lovage wiped her eyes with the back of her hand. "It doesn't matter now, because I don't think he loves me anymore. He feels betrayed by me, I think. He thinks I've been toying with his emotions."

Ginger just stood there, tears running slowly down her cheeks.

"Is that why you told people?" Lovage asked softly. "So it would get back to him? So it would cause trouble between us?"

"Ne!" Ginger's pretty little chin quivered. *"Ya..."* She hung her head. "I told some girls at Spence's. We were just talking and—" she took a breath "—it just came out." She rushed forward to take Lovage's hand. "I was so jealous that Marshall picked you, when I'd been trying to get him to ask me out for weeks and...and he was so handsome and the girls were talking about their beaus and...and I was jealous. Jealous of you, of them." She hung her head again. "I knew it might get back to him and I don't think I cared. Oh, Lovey, I'm so sorry. Please forgive me."

Lovage didn't know what to say. She was hurt that her sister had purposefully done something that could have potentially ruined her relationship with her beau, which it probably had. Lovage was upset that Ginger would cave in to the wickedness of gossip; their mother had taught them better. But she was also proud of Ginger for admitting her mistake. For asking for forgiveness, because God forgave His people for their sins. And didn't He teach that His people had to forgive each other, as well?

Ginger squeezed her hand. "And that happened weeks ago, and I didn't think you were serious about him, and I didn't—"

She began to cry in earnest then and Lovage put her arms around her.

"I'm so sorry," Ginger kept repeating. "It was a terrible thing I did. I can't believe I would do such a thing."

"Shh. It's all right," Lovage soothed, hugging her sister. "I forgive you."

"But it's not all right," Ginger wailed. "You said that Marshall doesn't want to see you anymore."

Lovage held tightly to Ginger, resting her head on her sister's shoulder. "Maybe it's for the best," she admitted, her voice quivering.

"*Ne, ne,* it's not. Not if you love him." She

drew back and looked up. "If you love him, you should fight for him. You should tell him that he mustn't let this come between you. Not if he loves you."

Lovage shook her head. She was crying again. "But maybe he doesn't," she whispered.

"Don't say that." Ginger set her jaw stubbornly. "Lovey, I know you have never thought any man would fall in love with and want to marry you, but I never believed that. You're the kindest, strongest woman I've ever known and I believe that any man who got to know you would want to marry you. And that goes for Marshall, too. He'd be a fool not to have fallen in love with you."

Lovage pushed hair that had fallen from her prayer *kapp* behind her ear. "It might be too late, Ginger," she said, the fight gone out of her. Now she just felt sad.

"It's not too late." Ginger grabbed her sister's hand. "I'll go to Marshall. I'll tell him exactly what I did and why I did it. I'll tell him how sorry I am and not to blame you." She wiped at her teary eyes. "I'll go right now." She started for the bathroom door.

"*Ne*, you won't." Lovage caught her elbow, stopping her. "You're going to go downstairs with me to set the table for supper and you're not going to speak a word of this to Mam. She doesn't need to worry herself over it."

"But I have to make it right," Ginger said fervently. "I have to go to him!"

"*Ne*, you won't go." Lovage slipped her arm around her sister's shoulders. "I don't want you involved. You've caused enough trouble."

"Oh, Lovey," she breathed, hugging her close. "He'll come to his senses. Marshall is a good man. He'll realize he made a mistake. And mark my words, I'll soon stand at your side on your wedding day."

Chapter Fourteen

Marshall walked into the small room off the tack room in the largest of his barns, where he kept his tools, and halted in the doorway. He gazed at the wall where an assortment of tools hung: hammers, screwdrivers, pliers, wrenches and saws, all sorted and displayed neatly on pegboards.

He pushed his straw hat back a bit and stared at the wall absently. He had no idea why he'd come into the tool room or what he needed.

With a sigh, he walked back out into the main area of the barn. The double doors that led out into the barnyard were open, allowing the crisp autumn air and sunshine to reach the darkest corners of the two-story structure. A couple of his grandmother's Guinea hens, which she gave full run of the farm, scratched in the clean straw outside the feed room. Lu, one of his milk cows, bellowed contentedly and he glanced in her direction. She'd had a run-in with a gatepost the previous week and had sustained a pretty big gash in her shoulder, so he was penning her up inside to keep her quiet. The wound was healing nicely, though, and he figured that in another day or two, he could let her back out with the other cows.

He walked over to the makeshift table he'd made with a piece of plywood and two wooden sawhorses he and Sam had built the previous year. He had removed the screen door from the back porch and laid it out on the table so he could repair or replace the screen. The day before, Petunia had broken through, trying to get to a bucket of scraps Grossmammi had left on the porch for Sam to add to the compost pile. Once Marshall had had a chance to survey the damage more closely, he had decided that the whole screen would have to be replaced. He'd retrieved a roll of galvanized screening from the shed, but that was far as he'd gotten. Now he needed rip out the old and put in the new.

That was the plan, at least, except that Marshall was feeling so scattered he couldn't concentrate on the project. He'd been like this for days. He kept starting tasks only to lose interest or energy. He continually misplaced objects; last night he'd spent ten minutes looking for his favorite pitchfork. The day before it had been his wool beanie. And sometimes he found himself standing somewhere with no idea why he was there or how he'd gotten there.

Petunia bleated and he looked up to see her standing in the open doorway, a leash dangling from the collar around her neck. He shook his head. The goat spent more time running loose than penned up. "Where's Sam?" he asked.

The goat didn't answer. Which made perfect sense. Marshall had been so grumpy for the last week that not even the pet goat wanted to be near him. Sam and Grossmammi had been steering clear of him, too.

Marshall was so miserable without Lovey. He didn't want to admit it at first, but it was true. He'd always been a positive type of person and she'd made him so happy. And now he wasn't. He missed her so much. Missed her smile. Missed talking to her. Missed just sitting beside her on the porch swing, so much that he didn't know which way was up. And he didn't know what to do about it.

Lovey had come to him Sunday after services to talk to him. She'd even admitted she'd gone out with him as a dare, but only that first time. What was he supposed to do with that information? He was so hurt. As he'd told her, he felt foolish. He could only imagine how many people—people he respected—were talking behind his back.

"Come on, girl," Marshall said to the goat. "You shouldn't be running around loose. That fox will eat you."

The goat took a step back and bleated at him again. With a sigh, Marshall moved quickly and grabbed the end of the leash just before Petunia could back out of his reach.

"Gotcha. Come on." He tugged on the leash and led her to her stall, which he and Sam had had to reinforce twice because she kept climbing over it. "Inside you go." He unclipped the leash and gave her a nudge. Then he dropped a soft, mealy apple from a bucket on the floor into a small trough on the other side, through a little hole in the door. It was another of Sam's inventions.

Petunia bleated one last protest and then began to munch on her apple.

Marshall walked back to the screen door, studied it for a minute and then remembered what he'd gone into the tool room for: shears. He walked to the room, grabbed the shears he used to cut metal and went back out to finish his task. To his surprise, he found his grandmother standing beside the table, studying the door.

"Can't fix the hole?" she asked.

"Ne." He pointed at the door with the shears. "That goat chewed it here. A patch won't hold. Especially not if she tries to get onto the porch again."

Lynita nodded and fingered Toby's leather halter, which was hanging on a post. Petunia had somehow managed to get ahold of it and he'd barely gotten it out of her mouth before she chewed it through. His *grossmammi* lifted it off the post and studied the chew marks.

"Also Petunia," he said irritably.

"It's in a goat's nature to chew things." She peered up at him. She was wearing a dark blue dress, a black prayer *kapp* and a pair of rubber shoes that made her look like she had duck feet. "Just like it's in the nature of a man to sulk."

It was obvious she was referring to him. "I'm not sulking." He set the shears down and started pulling away the rubber spline that held the screen in place in the groove.

She looked up at him. The October sun was bright enough that her transition sunglasses were dark. "Sam and I and the goat have had about enough of it." She hooked her thumb in the direction of Petunia's stall.

He frowned and tugged at the spline, thinking that if he didn't say anything, his grandmother would go away.

"You told me what happened with Lovage. The whole thing with her sister." She gave a wave of dismissal. "Silly girlish nonsense. You've taken it all too seriously."

He went on ripping out the spline; the screen came away with it.

Lynita rubbed the oiled leather of the halter between her fingers. "What you didn't say is what you were going to do about it."

"*Do* about it?" He kept his head down, avoiding her gaze. "Nothing to be done. It's over. She made a fool of me."

"Maybe, but now you're making a worse fool of yourself. First little problem that comes along and you give up?" she tsked. "And you think you're ready for marriage? I've got news for you, *sohn*. You marry any girl and you're going to come up on bigger logjams than this one."

Marshall grabbed the spline with his pliers, pulled too hard and it snapped, leaving a piece still partially embedded in the door. He groaned impatiently. "I thought you'd be happy. You didn't want me to marry Lovage. Faith's the girl you picked for me."

"True enough." Lynita gave a humorless laugh. "But you think I'm no better than that?"

"What do you mean?"

"Look at me," she said.

Slowly he lifted his gaze, until he looked down at her tiny face.

"What kind of grandmother do you think I am, that I'd be so set on a woman for my grandson I'd see him unhappy?" she demanded.

He stared at her, not quite comprehending what she was saying.

"*Sohn*, all I want is for you to live a Godly life and to be happy. For Sam to be happy. Would I have liked it if you had settled on Faith King? *Ya*, but you didn't." She shrugged. "You love that girl from New York? Then you better make this right. Because you won't be happy. You'll never be happy without her. And if *you're* not happy, *I'm* not happy."

His grandmother's words surprised him. He had just assumed she didn't like Lovage. That she was against him marrying her, plain and simple. "Make it right how?" he asked. "She played me."

"*Ya*, maybe. But then she apologized. She

cares for you, Marshall, and I think you care for her. You think you looked like a fool when those two girls played a little joke on you?" She waggled her finger at him. "You're going to look a bigger fool if you don't go to that girl, accept her apology and ask her to forgive you for not doing it days ago. Because let me tell you, a girl who can apologize for a mistake, those are few and far between. You better beg her for forgiveness and snatch her up fast."

Marshall set down his pliers. "You really think I should forgive her?"

"I think you better be asking her to forgive *you*." She frowned. And then she reached for the shears on the table and, to Marshall's astonishment, cut the noseband of Toby's halter right in half.

"What are you doing?" he asked, staring at the piece of tack in her hand.

She handed him the leather halter. "Needs fixing. You know a good harness shop?"

When Marshall pulled his wagon up in front of Benjamin Miller's place, he almost headed right back down the driveway. He was so nervous that his legs were wobbly as he walked through the shop door and the little bell jingled overhead. He was nervous and he was scared. Nervous because he wasn't sure what he was going to say to Lovey. Scared because what if he didn't say the right things? What if he had ruined everything, being so petty?

Over the top of a shelf, he spotted an Amish prayer *kapp*. A young woman was bent over the register, pushing buttons. When he came around the shelf, he saw that it was Lovey and he almost hightailed it for home. Instead, he strode toward her.

"How can I help—" When she saw who it was, she went quiet.

"Lovey," he murmured, sounding much calmer than he felt.

"Marshall," she breathed.

He couldn't look away from her. She was so beautiful in the midmorning light coming from a skylight overhead. Her blue dress was neatly pressed, her white apron and prayer *kapp* pristine. And she was watching him with the green eyes that had captivated him the first time they had met in this very same place.

"What— How can I help you?" she said, awkwardly setting her hands together on the counter.

"I, um…um…" He'd almost forgotten the halter his grandmother had purposely damaged to get him here. He held it up, dangling it from one finger.

She slowly moved her gaze to the piece of tack. "You came because you needed a halter repaired?" She sounded disappointed.

"*Ya*, I…" He closed his eyes. If he didn't find his nerve now, he never would. And as much as he dreaded this conversation, the possibility of living without Lovey was far worse. "*Ne*," he said firmly, opening his eyes. "This was an excuse. To see you." He dropped it on the counter. "Is Ginger here?"

"*Ya*. Working." She pointed to the door behind the counter. "In the back."

Without asking permission, Marshall pushed through the swinging half door beside the counter. And without permission, he grabbed Lovey's hand and led her to the back, flinging open the door and stepping into the workshop area. Spotting the little sister who had started this whole mess to begin with, seated at a sewing machine, he hollered, "Ginger!"

She looked up, startled, and lifted her foot off the treadle, bringing the needle to a standstill. "Marshall!" She looked scared.

"Go watch the cash register out front," he ordered, already starting to weave his way across the large workroom toward a door in the rear. "I need to talk to your sister privately."

Wide-eyed, Ginger flew off her stool. "Sure." She hurried toward the door to the shop. "Take as long as you want."

Still holding tightly to Lovey's hand, Marshall flung open the back door. Luckily, it actually led outside.

"Where are we going?" Lovey wasn't exactly protesting, but she was pulling back a little. Maybe trying to take her hand from his.

"Somewhere private," he told her. It had been his first thought to take her to the greenhouse he had built with her brothers. There, they could be alone, unseen, out of earshot. But a secluded place like that wasn't exactly the appropriate place for an unmarried couple to talk. They'd taken care to protect their reputations for three months; that wouldn't change now. Besides, it was too far away. Instead, he led her to the woodshed beside the old dairy barn that Benjamin had converted to his shop. He pulled her inside. The shed had three sides and was stacked to the ceiling with cords of wood for the woodstoves not just in the farmhouse, but the shop, as well. He stepped behind a neatly stacked pile of walnut.

"You should let go of my hand," she said, when they were facing each other.

"I'm not going to do that. Not until I've had my say."

She stood in front of him, her head bowed. But she hadn't taken her hand from his, not since they had stood at the cash register. And that gave him hope.

"Lovey, I came to apologize to you."

She lifted her head suddenly. "You did?" Her eyebrows knitted. They were the same color as her hair and neatly arched so that they framed her gorgeous green eyes. "For what?"

"For the mess I've made of things. For getting so upset about Ginger's dare. For caring what other men thought about me when I should have cared what *you* thought of me. For being embarrassed in front of the guys because of some silliness you had with your sister. Why do I care why you rode home with me from the softball game that night? All that matters is that you did." He looked down at the packed dirt floor of the woodshed; the shed smelled of sweet apple and pungent walnut. "It was foolish and prideful of me not to accept your apology on Sunday, Lovey. On Sunday of all days," he added.

She smiled at him, her gaze seeming to

search his. "I'm sorry I didn't tell you about the dare. Once I got to know you, I should have told you." She shrugged. "I guess I forgot about it. It just didn't seem all that important. Not once we started walking out together. Once I began to...care for you."

"You're right, it wasn't," he agreed.

She nibbled on her lower lip. "But I still should have told you."

He took her other hand so that he was clasping both of them. He had so much to say, words he hoped he would have a lifetime to share with her, but for now, he just wanted her to know how he felt. How much he cared for her. "Lovey, from that first day I walked into Benjamin's shop and saw you, I've been in love in you. I know I may seem lighthearted at times, but you have to believe me when I tell you I was never playing games with you. From that first ride home in my buggy when I asked you to marry me, I meant it, then and each and every time. I mean it now."

Tears filled Lovey's eyes and he squeezed her hands.

"I was never playing with your heart, either," she said, taking a step closer to him. Standing so close now that he could feel the warmth of her body and smell her honeysuckle shampoo. "Because I love you, too,

Marshall. So, *ya*, I'll marry you. But only if we can marry soon, because I don't think I can wait much longer to be your wife."

And then she shocked him by pressing her mouth to his as she held his gaze. Her kiss was so sweet, so tender, that Marshall's knees felt weak. And just when he feared he wouldn't ever be able to stop kissing her, he heard a peal of giggles. The two of them parted and turned to see Ginger, Nettie, Bay, Tara and Jesse all standing on the far side of the woodpile watching them, and he and Lovey laughed, too.

Epilogue

❧

Four Years Later

"Marshall! Elijah! Dinnertime," Lovage called from the steps of the screened-in porch.

"Coming," Marshall called, striding across the grass toward her. "We were in the orchard." He opened his arms wide to her. "Wait until you see how many Asian pears we have on the trees this year!"

She smiled and felt a little flutter in her chest that had been there since the first day she met him. "Where's Elijah?" she called. "He needs to wash up."

"Coming, Mam!" Their son, almost three years old now, burst out of the orchard and raced past his father.

Marshall scooped up the little boy, who

looked just like him but had her green eyes, and plopped him on his shoulders.

"Look at me!" Elijah called. He was dressed just like his father in dungaree jeans, a blue shirt, suspenders and a battered straw hat. He held his little hands high. "Look how big I am, Mam!"

"Just don't fall and crack your head like an egg," she warned. Then she looked to Marshall, who was grinning at her. She felt her cheeks grow warm. The Thursday in November almost four years ago when they had married, she thought she had loved him. But what she felt in her heart now was so much more. Her love for him had grown and matured beyond what she could possibly have imagined.

"Grossmammi and Sam have gone to the Grubers'," Lovage told Marshall. "I think he's sweet on May. He jumps at every invitation he can get out of the family." She held open the screen door for them.

"Where's Elsa?" Marshall asked, flashing her one of his handsome smiles.

"Napping." She sighed. "Thank goodness. I have a pile of ironing to do that's a mile high and she'd have no part of that this morning." She pointed to the table they kept on the porch most of the year round. It was their favorite place to eat. Here they were protected from the bugs and the sun and the wind, but in full view of their orchard, which was flowering now. "I'll be right back with the food." She looked up at their son on his father's shoulders.

Marshall lowered him to the porch floor and Elijah scooted past his mother and into the house.

"Sit down," Lovage told her husband, pointing to his chair at the table on the porch. "I've got everything on a tray to bring out. I just need to grab sugar."

"You want any help?"

"*Ne*. How are *your* hands?" she teased from the kitchen door.

He held them up, palms to her. "I washed at the barn because I knew better than to come to your table with dirty hands."

Lovage laughed and walked into the kitchen. First, she checked the baby, who, thankfully, was sound asleep in her little cradle Marshall had made with his own hands. Then she picked up a tray with ham sandwiches, broccoli slaw, potato salad and a measuring cup with sugar in it. "Hurry up, Elijah," she called in the direction of the downstairs bathroom. She could hear the water still running. "We'll wait for you."

Using her foot to open the door, Lovage

stepped out onto the porch, just in time to see Marshall lift a glass of lemonade to his mouth. He must have poured it for himself from the big glass pitcher in the center of the table.

"*Atch!* Don't—"

But it was too late. He took a big gulp of the fresh lemonade she'd just made, and his eyes got wide as he struggled to swallow.

"You've done it again," she said, trying not to laugh as she set down the tray and raised the measuring cup of sugar. She looked at the pitcher of lemonade and then at her husband. She couldn't help but laugh because his eyes were watering and his mouth puckered.

"I've done it again," he choked. And then he grabbed her by her hand and pulled her against him.

Lovage gave a little squeal. "Marshall, Elijah will—"

"Elijah will what?" Marshall asked, taking the cup of sugar from her and setting it back on the tray. "See that his parents love each other? Or that his mother's trying to poison his father?"

She sighed with happiness as he pulled her close, and she pressed her hand to his chest to look into his eyes. "I'll have you know, husband, that no one has ever died of unsweetened lemonade."

"*Ne?* Are you sure of that, wife?"

Marshall kissed Lovey on the mouth and she laughed as she tasted the sourness of the lemonade, and the sweetness of her life.

* * * * *

If you loved this book,
pick up these other stories of Amish life
from author Emma Miller's
previous miniseries
The Amish Matchmaker:

A Match for Addy
A Husband for Mari
A Beau for Katie
A Love for Leah
A Groom for Ruby

Available now from Love Inspired!

Find more great reads at
www.Harlequin.com.

Dear Reader,

Thank you for joining me in Hickory Grove, an Amish community just a stone's throw from Seven Poplars in Kent County, Delaware. Rosemary and Benjamin have their hands full with their new blended family, don't they? I suspect there will be bumps in the road, but the family's love for each other and their faith will see them through.

I hope you enjoyed Lovey and Marshall's story. Marshall had me worried there for a few minutes. Thank goodness his grandmother intervened. We all make mistakes sometimes and it takes a wise man or woman to accept our loved ones' shortcomings. I think Lovey and Marshall are perfect for each other, don't you?

I hope you'll join me in Hickory Grove again soon. I have a wonderful story of forgiveness to share with you when I introduce Benjamin's son Joshua to a newcomer, Phoebe. The love they find will truly warm your heart.

Until we meet again, friends.
I wish you peace and happiness.

Emma Miller

THE FORTUNES OF TEXAS COLLECTION!

18 FREE BOOKS in all!

Treat yourself to the rich legacy of the Fortune and Mendoza clans
in this remarkable 50-book collection. This collection is packed with
cowboys, tycoons and Texas-sized romances!

YES! Please send me **The Fortunes of Texas Collection** in Larger Print.
This collection begins with 3 FREE books and 2 FREE gifts in the first
shipment. Along with my 3 free books, I'll also get the next 4 books from
The Fortunes of Texas Collection, in LARGER PRINT, which I may either
return and owe nothing, or keep for the low price of $5.24 U.S./$5.89 CDN
each plus $2.99 for shipping and handling per shipment*. If I decide to
continue, about once a month for 8 months I will get 6 or 7 more books but
will only need to pay for 4. That means 2 or 3 books in every shipment will
be FREE! If I decide to keep the entire collection, I'll have paid for only 32
books because 18 books are FREE! I understand that accepting the 3 free
books and gifts places me under no obligation to buy anything. I can always
return a shipment and cancel at any time. My free books and gifts are mine
to keep no matter what I decide.

☐ 269 HCN 4622   ☐ 469 HCN 4622

Name (please print)

Address   Apt. #

City   State/Province   Zip/Postal Code

Mail to the **Reader Service:**
IN U.S.A.: P.O. Box 1341, Buffalo, N.Y. 14240-8531
IN CANADA: P.O. Box 603, Fort Erie, Ontario L2A 5X3

READERSERVICE.COM

Manage your account online!

- Review your order history
- Manage your payments
- Update your address

*We've designed the
Reader Service website
just for you.*

Enjoy all the features!

- Discover new series available to you, and read excerpts from any series.
- Respond to mailings and special monthly offers.
- Browse the Bonus Bucks catalog and online-only exculsives.
- Share your feedback.

Visit us at:

ReaderService.com

RS16R